I0547437

BELONG TO ME

AN EROTIC ROMANCE

JENNIFER PROBST

This is a work of fiction. Names, characters, organizations, places, events, and incidents are either products of the author's imagination or are used fictitiously.

Text copyright © 2025 by Triple J Publishing Inc.

ISBN (print) 979-8-9909913-6-1

All rights reserved.

No part of this book may be reproduced, or stored in a retrieval system, or transmitted in any form or by any means, electronic, mechanical, photocopying, recording, or otherwise, without express written permission of the publisher.

Cover design by Hang Le

PRAISE FOR JENNIFER
PROBST AND HER NOVELS:

Praise for Jennifer Probst and her novels:

"There's a reason Probst is the gold-standard in contemporary romance." —**Lauren Layne,** *New York Times* **bestselling author**

"Jennifer Probst knows how to bring the swoons and the sexy!" —**Amy Reichert, author of** *The Coincidence of Coconut Cake*

"Probst is one of the best contemporary romance authors I know!" —**Angela Carr, Under the Covers blog**

Praise for the Steele Brothers series:

"Rome is a Dominant God and Sloane is a feisty yet submissive match for him." —**NYT & USA Today Bestselling Author, CD Reiss**

"Beg Me is a wonderful mix of sexy and sweet. Hot loving and a wonderful second chance story line make for an amazing story. I devoured Beg Me in one sitting. Rem and Cara steam up the pages, but it's their love story that really kept me hooked. Open and honest, everyone can relate to these characters." **—NYT & USA Today Bestselling Author, Lexi Blake**

"Sweet and incredibly hot, you'll want to grab this bright and richly decadent fantasy come to life." **—NYT Bestselling Author, Kendall Ryan**

OTHER BOOKS BY JENNIFER PROBST

A Brand New Ending

Something Just Like This

Begin Again

The Billionaire Builders Series

Everywhere and Every Way

Any Time, Any Place

Somehow, Some Way

All or Nothing at All

The Searching . . . Series

Searching for Someday

Searching for Perfect

Searching for Beautiful

Searching for Always

Searching for You

Searching for Mine

Searching for Disaster

The Marriage to a Billionaire Series

The Marriage Bargain

The Marriage Trap

The Marriage Mistake

The Marriage Merger

The Marriage Arrangement

The Book of Spells

The Marriage Arrangement

The Steele Brothers Series

Catch Me

Play Me

Dare Me

Beg Me

Reveal Me

Sex on the Beach Series

Beyond Me

Chasing Me

The Hot in the Hamptons Series

Summer Sins

Stand-Alone Novels

Dante's Fire

Executive Seduction

Unbreak my Heart

The Grinch of Starlight Bend

Love Me Anyway

All For You

For Writers

Write Naked: A Bestseller's Secrets to Writing Romance &
Navigating the Path to Success

Write True: A Bestseller's Guide to Writing Craft and Achieving
Success in the Romance Industry

Writers Inspiring Writers: What I'd Wish I'd Known

TO MY READERS

To My Reader,

I loved writing Belong to Me. Start with a delicious concept: masked strangers and a bargain to be truthful. Add in the mystery of never revealing their faces, and the stark intimacy of sharing every secret fantasy. The result is a steamy romance that breaks down all barriers. I feel that readers can relate to this couple who have to battle their fear of vulnerability in order to win the ultimate prize: love.

I truly hope you enjoy the journey and I look forward to sharing more stories.

Please note this book was originally published and entitled, *Masquerade*. It has been updated with additional scenes, new cover, and new title.

CHAPTER ONE

HAILEY ASHTON CLOSED the door to her best friend's office and sat down on the chair opposite his desk. Her fingers trembled slightly with excitement as she slid the gold embossed invitation across the polished wood. "I'm going to meet the man of my dreams."

Theodore Rivers raised one brow at her declaration and picked up the invitation. "I didn't know you were looking for one."

"Who isn't? We may have changed our standards from slaying dragons to doing dishes, but it's still a lifelong quest."

He grinned and glanced at the card. "A masquerade ball?"

Hailey leaned over. "It's the annual party our boss sponsors. I've heard stories about them but I've never gone."

"Yeah, I remember seeing one of these in my mailbox. I've never gone either. It's more like a weekend event than a party. He invited the higher-up employees but mostly the rich and famous attend. He picks a different theme each year. This one's being held on his private island. Must be nice." Theodore narrowed golden brown eyes. "Don't tell me. You've targeted some Duke of England to take you away from all this."

"Very funny. I don't care about money and you know it. I just thought this would be different." She paced the wood floors, her heels clicking steadily. "Sometimes I feel like my life is closing in on me. I do everything right. I exercise at the gym, I don't eat red meat, I make sure I get eight hours sleep. Even the men I date are boring. Do you know I can't remember the last time a man kissed me good night and I wanted more? Usually I can't wait to get back to my own apartment. Lord, I have more fun with you watching Netflix and eating popcorn. Isn't that sad?"

"Tragic," he said wryly.

"Sorry, I didn't mean it like that." She sighed and brushed back a stray red curl from her forehead. "I want to break out of my routine and meet someone I've always wondered about."

Theodore studied her, then shifted in his chair. The leather creaked gently beneath his weight. "Are you looking for a general man of your dreams, or have you narrowed the search to one?"

Unfortunately, he knew her well enough to realize she hid something. "I'd confess but you'll probably yell."

He muttered something under his breath. "Tell me."

"Promise you won't lecture?" she asked.

He groaned. "I promise. Spill it."

"Our boss."

His face plainly showed his disbelief. "You're kidding me. Ciro Demitris? He's not only the boss of this company, Hailey. He owns a software empire all over the world and he's probably richer than Bezos. You've never even met him. Hell, most people in the organization never caught a glance of the guy."

She raised her chin. "I've seen his pictures! I'd know what he looks like if I saw him."

Theodore shook his head. "You think this man is the

answer to your rut? He'd eat you for breakfast and not look back."

Her voice turned to ice. "Thanks for the confidence in me."

"Oh, hell, you know what I meant. The rumors about him should make you think twice. Why do you think he throws these parties each year? He's an eccentric who likes to play with people's minds. He does this for his own entertainment."

"You know nothing about him personally, and neither do I. But this party can change that. I know you don't think I'm glamorous enough to hold my own, but with a mask on I can be the woman I always wanted. I can be beautiful and exciting and mysterious."

His tone softened as he stared at her. "You always were, Hailey. You just don't see it."

She stopped pacing and looked down at her sensible oatmeal colored business suit and pumps. As always, she dressed to be a businesswoman, and she realized that somehow, along the way, the real woman inside had gotten lost. How could she explain to anyone, even her best friend? She walked back over to the chair and sank down. Then tried to put her feelings into words.

"I'm thirty years old, Theodore. I've never been married, never had children, and until lately, I never thought I'd miss it. But I feel trapped. I'm afraid to do anything different if it doesn't fit with my daily schedule. I live for my work, but I know there has to be more out there. This is a chance to see. And even if nothing happens between us, at least I know I tried. Can you understand?"

A strange array of emotions passed over his carved features, then cleared. He smiled. "Yeah, I think I understand. But these parties are way out of your league. Demitris is known for his erotic themes. I've heard stories about drunken orgies, people playing out their sexual fantasies.

Anything goes when a person steps through the door. He's made a reputation of being entirely discreet, and offering his guests the same." Theodore paused. "I'm worried."

Hailey faced her best friend and realized she couldn't tell him the whole truth. He was the only man she felt close to, but had never confessed her upbringing. She wasn't one to blame her sexual restrictions on her parents, though their forceful belief sex was wrong had caused problems with intimacy since her teens.

She spent most of her life being reminded of her mother's mistake. Namely her. One drunken night had produced her parent's only child, and after they were forced to marry, they turned to religion to right their wrong. Sex was wrong. Sex meant loss of control, loss of a rightful path in life. Sex meant diseases and pregnancy and a man controlling every part of a woman's existence. Sex meant less choices. Pleasure lasted a few moments, and her parents made sure she would never pay with a future of limitations for one reckless night. Of course, she had rebelled just once.

Then realized her parents were right.

Hailey firmly shook off the memory and re-focused on Theo. She ached for an experience to finally propel her out of her routine. She wanted to finally be free to express her sexuality without fear. The idea of shedding her clothes and her prim ways left her with a tingle of heat that bloomed in her belly. An odd combination of wanting and shame mingled together. She battled constantly with an inner voice that taunted, its familiar sensual tone urging her to throw away constraints.

The voice came sometimes in the middle of the night, a swirl of sexual images of naked men in a tangle of limbs, sucking at her breasts, thrusting their fingers deep inside of her as she screamed for release. The dreams were relentless, until she would wake in the middle of the night, bucking her hips upward into empty space, the tension pounding through her body until she moaned in agony and waited for the feeling to pass. With an iron-willed control, she never let herself go, never pleasured herself.

How many times had she tried with a vibrator? Desperation pushed her to experiment with letting go of her inhibitions, but something inside her immediately shut down the moment she began to near orgasm.

Yes, she was messed up. She'd thought about going to a sex therapist but hadn't taken the leap. Hailey had grown up with an overpowering need to control her life to the last detail, which included her sexuality. Much easier to deny the wanting then pass over the edge of no return. Because the voice that came to her deep in the darkness always reminded her once she plummeted into her sexual fantasies, she'd never come back.

But the voice was growing stronger. She'd always been able to keep the echo to a low murmur. Now, the roar crashed through her mental barriers at night and left her aching for so much more.

She admitted to obsessing a bit over Ciro Demitris. Once she'd seen his picture in the company's quarterly newsletter, something had clicked inside. Looking into those stunning blue eyes, something had happened to her. The article in Fortune magazine sketched him as a private eccentric who lived an isolated life. He was well-known for his sexual appetites—talking openly that sex should be a way to achieve pleasure, and there was no right or wrong way. It was in exact contradiction to her parents' beliefs. Since she saw Ciro, she'd been dreaming of him nightly and how he could eventually free her.

Hailey wanted him to be the one to do all the things she fantasized about. She didn't want to be afraid any longer of losing control.

She sensed he'd be experienced enough to know what to do. Maybe he'd even see her as a challenge. Her instincts screamed he was the one meant for her, and this time, Hailey intended to follow her gut. When the invite arrived, she knew the time had come to take a chance.

Her life was perfect on paper. Strong financial background. Solid career path. The ability to choose any path she craved. Yet, she felt unfulfilled and empty as she moved through her days. She admitted she was now more scared of being trapped in her ideal life than she was of embarking on a reckless affair.

Theodore was her safety net. The friend who had her back, in work and in her personal life. He was sweet, and supportive. But he'd never understand her hidden dark fantasies, or the struggle to finally be free.

"I'll be fine." She said the words firmly but a quiver in her belly screamed she was a liar.

He nodded, obviously deciding to accept her decision. "Okay. So, what's the plan?"

"I already know where I can rent my costume and mask. The party starts Thursday night, and ends Sunday. Everyone unmasks at dawn on the final night. The map was enclosed with the invitation so I know how to get there." She brightened. "Why don't you come with me? This party could help you, too."

He winced. "Boy, you're full of complements this morning. I happen to be satisfied with my dull life."

"You need a woman, old friend. I think your last date was six months ago, almost the same time mine was," she teased.

"Sorry, the Bulls game is on. No glamour queen can compete."

"You're still hung up on her, aren't you?" she asked softly.

He stiffened, then consciously relaxed his fingers around the invitation. "My faithless ex-wife is off having a grand old time with her boyfriend. I never give her a second thought."

"It's been two years, Theodore."

He gave a lopsided grin, full of his usual charm. "She

never let me watch the basketball games. How could I possibly miss her?"

She let him coax a smile from her. "Okay, I give. I should know by now you'll never be one of these tortured heroes like Heathcliff in Wuthering Heights. I've got to stop forcing that role on you."

"Deal," he said. He glanced at his watch. "I've got a meeting at ten. Davidson has a new software program he's still working kinks out of and my head's on the block. Our charming

boss will fire me in a heartbeat if I don't get it working. Hmmm, maybe if you two hit it off you can put in a good word for me."

"Cute, real cute." She paused, then bit her lip as she tried to broach the subject. "Theodore, I've got to ask you for one small favor."

He rubbed his fingers against his temple as if anticipating a headache. Black strands of hair ruffled under the motion, then settled back into place. "Why am I afraid to ask?"

"Well, since it's a masquerade ball, and you so intelligently pointed out I don't really know what our boss looks like, I need to know what he'll be wearing."

He blinked. "There's going to be hundreds of people in that mansion. All in masks and costumes. How am I supposed to get this information?"

"Oh, come on, you've got the inside on all the top people in this firm. We both know this party is presented as a social occasion, but it's still about business. Executives are going to want to get the ear of Ciro Demitris. I bet there are people who'll know exactly what his costume is. I just need you to be one of them."

"You don't ask for much. Just the impossible."

She grinned cheekily. "Use your charm. That's why you've been promoted to Director, isn't it?"

"And your smart comebacks are why you're still a lowly manager."

She made a face, then rose from the chair and walked towards the door. "So, this wonderful manager can count on her best friend to do a little detective work, right?"

The phone beeped insistently and interrupted his comeback. He reached for the receiver and mouthed, "You owe me."

She laughed and left the office.

HAILEY STARED AT THE WOMAN IN THE FULL-LENGTH MIRROR and caught her breath. It was her. But it wasn't.

The woman's hair had been left loose instead of fastened into her usual tight bun. Gleaming red strands poured wildly down her shoulders. Her blue eyes were framed by dark, lush lashes and took on a hint of mystery behind the brightly colored peacock mask. Her lips had been lined and colored with deep red lipstick, making them appear full and enticing. Her conservative suits and baggy sweat pants had been thrown away and replaced with a midnight blue silk dress. The material covered every inch of her body but slashed down the front in a deep V, exposing the ripe white curves of her breasts. Delicate high heeled sandals enhanced her height. A simple strand of diamonds clasped around her neck, and the light caught and shimmered on the stones, emphasizing the smooth naked skin beyond.

The longer she stared at her reflection, the more she felt as if a change was taking place deep inside of her. Tonight was the opportunity to explore hidden parts of herself she had denied. She dated many men before, but always approached the relationship with a brick wall firmly erected to hide her feelings. Usually after the third date, the man realized he wasn't going to get "lucky" and moved on. Hailey admitted a portion of fault. She never gave them a chance to get to know her. She offered intelligent conversation, the occasional humor, and a simple elegance that was part of her nature. Never any raw emotions or vulnerability.

God, how she wanted that now. How she wanted to experience a man who could think of nothing but touching her skin; giving pleasure. A man who was so forceful there would be no thought to holding back. Poised on the edge of a cliff, Hailey wanted more than anything to take a deep breath and jump. But she was still afraid she couldn't.

Therefore, Ciro Demitris was the perfect man. A man who might give her the push she so desperately needed.

She intended to find the man behind the public image. He was confident about his abilities and could have any woman he wanted. He showed a cool demeanor to the world, but Hailey suspected he felt a number of things kept carefully hidden. The magazine article painted him as a corporate mogul who traveled the globe and dated a variety of beautiful women.

Hailey was more interested in the private man, the one who gave to charities and avoided long term commitments, possibly because of a broken heart. Like Theodore did.

The thought made her check her phone. Still no text. She needed to leave within the hour and he still hadn't called. There was no way her plan could work if she didn't know what her boss wore.

The phone rang.

She snatched it up. "Did you get the information?"

A deep laugh rumbled in her ear. "No hello? No singing 'Hail to the Hero' when I risked my life to get you the identity of his top-secret costume? No sweet reward?"

She sighed impatiently. "You're impossible. I promise when I come back, I'll personally give you what you want."

"You know how that sounded, right?"

"Theodore!"

"Fine. Our tycoon will be the Phantom of the Opera this evening. Fitting, too. The guy seems to be part mystery, part monster."

"Thank you. You don't know how much this means to me," she said.

The line hummed with sudden silence. When he spoke, his voice was quiet. "I think I do. I hope you find what you're looking for tonight."

"I hope so too," she whispered. "Bye. I'll call you on Sunday when I get back."

"I'll be waiting."

Hailey hung up.

———

THEODORE GLANCED AT HIS PACKED SUITCASE. TENSION twisted his gut when he realized there would be no turning back. The plan was set. He had imparted the identity of the costume, and now Hailey was poised to meet the man who would turn her sexual fantasies into reality.

The only thing she didn't know was the man would be Theodore Rivers, not Ciro Demitris.

The thought of finally touching her the way he craved made him grow hard. Yes, he was her best friend. But he wanted so much more, and every time he dared to push the line, he watched her back off with a polite wariness that stopped him like a bucket of ice water. She would never give him a chance. He lived with the knowledge for almost a year now, and he finally had the opportunity to change his future. Their future.

Two years ago, they were working on the same project together and formed a tentative friendship. An attraction always zinged beneath the surface, but he'd been married, and committed to his wife.

Until his wife left him. Admitted to an affair and walked off without a glance back.

Things began to fall apart at work and in all aspects of his life. He refused to admit he needed help, but Hailey had saved his ass on many occasions and never asked a question. Before long, they were spending more time together. Drinks after work; planning sessions spent in the dim light of the conference room; long lunches over a bottle of wine. He finally opened up and told her everything. She held his hand as he cried for the first time. She supported him through lonely evenings and made him laugh again.

Theodore dragged in a breath and thought over the past year they spent together. He couldn't pinpoint the moment he fell in love with her. He believed it was a gradual deepening of emotion. Slow and steady rather than hot and fast.

Before long, they were having movie nights together with a tub of popcorn, feet propped up on the table clad in comfortable sweatpants. They took tennis lessons and teased each other over their bumbling inaccuracies and lack of coordination. He didn't remember when he stopped grieving his wife and looked toward the future. A future he wanted to share with Hailey.

Theodore began to pace. He'd been officially friend-zoned and cock-blocked. To much time had passed before he realized he wanted her naked and in his arms. He watched her date a variety of men with a knot in his gut. At least, she rarely got past a few dates. The man would always demand a certain level of intimacy, and Hailey would come back to him; her safe, comfortable friend. But whenever he felt courageous enough to take their relationship to the next level, he sensed the distance within her and he always backed off.

She'd never let him be her lover.

Hailey was too comfortable in their routine to risk a change. Too comfortable taking a chance and ruining their friendship. She wanted the safety of their relationship and the guarantee she'd never be asked for more.

He cursed under his breath. Hailey was his other half. So eager to control all aspects of her life, that life began to control her. He'd pursued the same path after his wife left him. But now he wanted Hailey enough to take a leap – even if it meant losing her forever.

Theodore knew she was afraid to let go, and admitted he became intrigued by becoming the man to tap into those hidden parts. Her body screamed sex, but her aura kept men firmly away. Soon, the friendship became torture, until he'd leave her home in an agony of sexual frustration, with no way to get what he wanted.

Until now.

He'd noticed a change in her the past few weeks. A restless gleam within those sky blue eyes; a distraction in her work. He watched her talk with other men and found she was more open; more flirtatious. Like a juicy fruit on the vine, Hailey was ready to be picked; savored; eaten. After all the years of celibacy, she'd reached her explosion point. Rage wrenched at him when he heard of her plan. He'd lose her. Somehow, she was finally ready to take a chance and explore her sexuality, but not with Theo.

Instead, she'd picked a stranger with a heartless reputation who would use her and throw her away. Theodore did not intend for that to happen. If his lady wanted to be seduced and fucked, he planned to give her exactly what she wanted.

On his terms.

Theo stopped pacing and stared in the mirror. The stage was set. He'd studied Demitris' photo and carefully changed enough of his appearance to his satisfaction. Contact lenses turned his brown eyes to blue. He'd slicked his hair back away from his face in the style that made Ciro famous for female fantasies, and pierced his left ear with one diamond earring. His cloak and mask would cover his body, though he was similar height and weight.

But he knew more than his appearance needed to change.

Theodore shook his head when he thought of the past year and his behavior. He always played the protector, not the seductor. This weekend would give him the opportunity to slip into a more dominant role. Demitris was a loner. Probably a control freak. Used to getting women and weary of the games they played. He would take all of those elements and use them for the role. Hailey confessed she wanted to be free to become a different woman.

He intended to be a different man.

Hailey expected the billionaire and wouldn't search for similarities to her safe, dull friend. He felt confident she wouldn't recognize him. The rest he'd leave to Fate.

Theo switched off the lights. He knew Hailey would never give him the opportunity to please her. The need was always a distant glimmer in her blue eyes, a need he intended to satisfy this weekend. And when it was all over, and he unmasked, if she turned him away at least he would have the memory of her to warm the cold nights ahead. The memory of her breasts in his mouth; his dick thrust deep inside her heat; her screams echoing in his ear. Anything was worth that.

Anything.

CHAPTER TWO

HAILEY REACHED the mansion after sundown.

She looked up in wonderment at the white washed stucco gleaming under the first splash of moonlight. Set on a hill, surrounded by palm trees and thick vegetation, it reminded her of a place out of a fantasy. Multiple decks hooked around the first and second story, offering visitors an enthralling view of the beach. Hailey breathed in the fragrant air scented with exotic florals, picking her way over the curving pathway. The sounds of laughter, music, and the crash of waves caressed her ears and called to her as if in a dream. She paused at the steps and took in the scene before her.

People gathered on the decks and throughout the gardens, sipping champagne. Colorful masks and brilliant costumes filled her vision and added to the dreamlike quality. And she realized for the first time, she could explore the real Hailey Ashton, who was safely hidden behind her mask and would not have to be exposed until the final night.

She grabbed a glass of champagne and made her way deeper into the gardens, seeking a moment to gather her composure. Erotic statues scattered the grounds amidst a Koi Pond and several waterfalls. A few people bumped her from behind, pushing her forward. She glanced around, trying to be brave, and wondered how she was going to find him. The man could be anywhere.

Maybe she'd go inside the house and explore each floor. Work her way up and search every room, even though there may be a hundred. If she focused on—

Someone was watching her.

Hailey spun around. She searched through the flickering lights and dancing shadows. Her skin tingled and burned, as if touched by the sun. A whirl of masked faces blurred her vision as she began to walk, slightly stumbling over the hem of her dress. The music surrounded her along with dim shouts of laughter and gaiety, and then her gaze caught on a flash of white which pierced through the darkness.

He stood on the balcony overlooking the garden. A black cloak covered his body. His hair was slicked back from his forehead, the strands inky black and blending with the darkness. Catlike eyes gleamed through the carved holes of the stark white mask.

Hailey sucked in her breath as a current of raw, sexual energy sizzled in the air. Most of his face was covered, leaving only his mouth and eyes exposed. But as her gaze met his, Hailey felt his isolation as he stood alone, watching her. Dressed as the Phantom, he was a man who kept to the shadows, presenting a civilized veneer to the world which masked the violence, and Hailey knew then she gazed upon Ciro Demitris.

Minutes ticked by. Frozen by the sheer power of the electricity crackling between them, Hailey waited, torn between the need to flee and the need to stay, as their eyes met and locked.

Then he turned and with a sweep of his cloak, disappeared from the balcony.

Hailey shuddered. The tension eased, and she began to

re-gather her control. This was what she had come for, but the reality of his presence shook her to the very core.

Fantasies were one thing while safe in her bed. But the reality challenged all her fears, especially when seeing Ciro in person.

For a few moments, her brain shouted all the ways this could be the biggest mistake of her life.

With a deep breath, she shut off the distracting thoughts and decided tonight would all be about action.

Find him before he disappears again.

She headed determinedly through the garden. She found the staircase and made her way to the second floor, hoping he'd still be up there. She passed couples lounging on the steps. A woman with her gown pulled down to the waist laughed as the man beside her dribbled champagne over her breasts and licked at her nipples. Her moans mingled with the strains of the music. Hailey rushed past them, face burning, and walked down the dimly lit hallway. The chattering voices and music grew faint when she finally found the balcony where her host had stood. The doors were flung open, and Hailey glimpsed the twisting pathways of the garden in the distance. The bedroom was decorated in wood and burgundy tones. She caught the faint scent of musk and spice from the room's last occupant.

He wasn't there.

Hailey sighed and turned away. Maybe he decided to join the party in the ballroom. She still didn't know how she would approach him, what she would say...

"You shouldn't have come."

A deep masculine voice cut through the air. Steel sheathed in silk. Satin dragged over skin. A gravelly tone, yet oddly familiar. Vivid images flashed before her as Hailey felt that voice pour over her ears like warm honey, and her body responded as if the heavy liquid had been dripped over the naked breasts; hips; thighs.

Her hand paused on the knob. Halfway tempted to flee, she forced herself to turn and reminded herself this man was whom she had crossed an ocean to meet.

He stepped out of the shadows. His black cloak whispered around his body as he moved toward her. Hailey ignored her rapidly beating heart and strived to sound cool and confident.

"I'm sorry, I didn't know anyone was in here," she said as he drew closer. "I was so intrigued by the villa I decided to do a little exploring."

Those eyes narrowed, and Hailey realized they were not just regular blue, but a dark navy with sparks of gold. Like the deep depths of the ocean meeting the sparkle of sunlight. The odd combination made his gaze even more haunting. His lips turned downward in a sneer. "Forgive me for assuming we'd start by being honest. I've forgotten how easy it is for women to lie."

She flinched in both surprise and embarrassment. Hailey forced her chin upward. "I don't lie. And I resent your assumptions about my character. You don't even know who I am."

"I know you came looking for me," he said softly. "I know we're about to start the game a man and woman play when they're attracted to one another. But it's not time yet." He turned as if to dismiss her. "I'm not ready to join the others. You shouldn't have come," he repeated.

An outraged squeak escaped her lips at his raging arrogance. "You flatter yourself, Phantom. I came up here for my own reasons. Now that you've satisfied my curiosity, I can leave." Hailey spun on her heel and opened the door. The music drifted through the crack and filled the room.

"So, you did lie."

She stiffened. "I suppose I did. But you're safe from me. I'm not interested in playing games."

His voice was rough and demanding. "Then what did you want?"

Hailey refused to turn around, refused to meet those mocking eyes. "I saw a man who was lonely. Separate. I came up here to find out what could cause someone to feel like that." She paused. "Now I know."

She shut the door behind her. On the stairs, the bare breasted woman thrust upward to receive the ministrations of her lover. The man flicked his fingers over one juicy red nipple, then bent his head. She closed her eyes in delight.

Hailey rushed past them and stopped in the ballroom. Tears burned behind her eyelids but she refused to give in. She had been wrong. She wanted to meet Ciro Demitris, but he was too beyond her, too ensnared in these wicked sexual games that she couldn't seem to play. Theodore was right. She was way out of her league.

Hailey grabbed a glass of champagne and took a few healthy swallows. Though repulsed by his arrogant statements, the pounding heat between her thighs was still too real. He excited her with his command; his masculinity; the raw heat shimmering in those blue-gold eyes. She tried to fight the vivid picture swirling past her of what she could do with the Phantom. Tried

to ignore how badly she wanted to be the bare breasted woman being pleasured.

She thought of leaving, but why let Demitris win? The party could still strip away her restrictions and allow her to express some freedom.

Her heels clicked on the highly polished marble floors as she explored the mansion. A twelve-piece orchestra took up the front part of the room, and couples danced to old classics like Glen Miller and Frank Sinatra. Men in dark suits and tuxedos escorted women dressed in rich velvets and shimmering satin, hidden by a variety of masks that enticed as much as they concealed. A mingling rush of perfumes and sweat wafted through the air.

A crystal chandelier sparkled above as she walked through the ballroom. Long banquet tables were filled with every type of food imaginable, so she tried some caviar for the first time, and indulged in tiny bite sized morsels cooked to perfection. The walls were filled with gorgeous watercolors and art work she immediately knew were priceless. A circular staircase reminded her of the old southern style in Gone with the Wind, when Rhett Butler first spotted the beautiful Scarlett.

The champagne helped. Suddenly, a stranger pulled her into his arms and swept her across the floor. She opened her mouth to protest, but as the music swelled, she gave herself to the moment. The sweet fire of alcohol heated her blood. One man's arms led to another as she danced with a long line of suitors, and looked into faces hidden by masks.

Something inside of her loosened and broke through her normal reserve. As the hours ticked toward midnight, the music changed to a grinding, sexy hip hop; pounding and pulsing in a more demanding rhythm. Hailey swung from partner to partner. She threw back her head and relished in the freedom of the moment, and then someone's arms were catching her again, and she was pulled toward a broad chest and held in an iron grip.

His gaze burned with a masculine demand behind a gleaming white mask. Hailey stumbled, and her fingers automatically gripped the sleek folds of his cloak as she fought for balance. He drew her closer until every carved muscle of his body pressed against hers. The demanding thrust of his cock settled between her thighs. Her stomach dipped as liquid heat pulsed in demand.

She tried to fight the demands of her body. Heavy, tender breasts. Tight nipples rising to greet him and be freed. Heart beating rapidly in her chest.

Hailey shuddered. "Why did you come?"

A smile touched his lips. His jaw held rough stubble and gave him a more dangerous air. The diamond in his left ear caught the light and glimmered with icy brilliance. "Curiosity. You haven't satisfied it yet."

Fear flamed to life. Hailey wondered if he spotted the emotion in her face. "I'm not part of your fantasy, Phantom. I'll dance with you, but I won't play your games."

"Then you're lying to yourself, sweetness. The moment you put on the mask and stepped through the gates you told me you wanted to play." His fingers trailed the length of her spine in a gentle caress, which contradicted the hardness in his eyes. "That's what you're here for."

"And what are you here for?" she asked. "You sit in judgement, hiding behind a cloak and a mask while you watch and wait. It's easy to be cynical of life when you refuse to be in it, Phantom. Perhaps that's your own secret fear."

Another man reached out to grab her. Demitris twisted her around to avoid the outstretched arms, and his black cloak swirled around their legs as she was led to the other side of the room.

"You've got a sharp tongue," he said.

"And you're arrogant."

Did his face reflect surprise or was that a trick of the light? Hailey wondered if there was anyone who surprised him. Something told her he had lived so long in the shadows, he didn't know anything else existed.

"I don't know if I believe you," he said. "It could be clever words and a clever act. Lies mesh too easily with truth when people play games, and women know that better than anyone."

"You're also a chauvinist," she told him pleasantly.

"Maybe you know who I am. Maybe you decided to play with fire because you feel safe behind a mask."

Hailey nodded. "Maybe you're right."

"Who are you?" he demanded.

She stared at him through the carved eyeholes. She had come tonight to be a different person, but suddenly, she wanted to give him the truth of who she was. For once, safe behind her mask, she wanted to reveal herself to him in a way she never had before. The possibility of such surrender made fear curl and tighten in her stomach. Along with excitement.

"My name is Hailey."

"What do you want?"

She took a deep breath and plunged. "I want to know you. The person behind the mask, the person inside. And I want you to know me."

"People never reveal their true selves. They conceal and lie until they don't know who they are anymore." His tone held distance; pain. "They only want what they perceive, and when they find the truth, they leave."

"I want to know you," she repeated.

He suddenly gripped her arm and dragged her off the dance floor. He turned her around and pointed to the couple on the stairs who writhed in delight. The man had now shoved up the woman's gown, and her legs lay open to any observer, her pussy pink and wet as the man slid his finger over her. Her cries were swallowed up in the roar of the crowd.

Hailey felt the strength of his rock-hard erection strain against her buttocks. Felt his fingers clamp around her arms. She stiffened, trying to mask her response. Her mind fought the knowledge her body already embraced. She wanted this man, wanted to be claimed by him.

"Do you see them, Hailey?" His voice was a low growl of sound. He slowly pulled her back against him. Lifted her up an inch. Then rocked into her with slow, subtle motions. "That's what you came here for tonight. And I intend to give you everything you want. But first we set up the rules of the game."

"What rules?"

"You'll tell me everything. No lies, no half-truths, no denials. You must lay yourself bare and open as that woman's legs, and let me do whatever I want to you. You'll answer every one of my questions. Obey my every command for the whole time you're here. And on the last night, I'll let you choose. You can walk away without ever seeing my face. Or you can unmask and I will do the same."

Her body shook. Her gaze was trained on the couple. She struggled to draw air into her lungs. "I have to give you everything?" Hailey repeated.

"Everything."

She paused. Then craned her head around to face him. "Why make a bargain with me? There's plenty of women here who'll do whatever you want without hesitation."

A half smile settled on his full lips. "Because you came looking for me. You made me want you."

She closed her eyes and tried to clear her head. Tried to think of the implications of such a bargain. "I did no such thing and you still didn't answer the question. You want more than just one night of sex. You want..."

"I want it all." Her eyes flew open. He pulled her harder against him and forced his cock between her ass cheeks until she fell forward, unbalanced. Forced her to breathe in the masculine scents of musk and spice and soap; to cradle his iron hard thighs. Forced her to imagine those carved lips taking his pleasure over her body; to match each demanding thrust of his tongue and still ask for more.

"Aren't you tired of hiding? When was the last time you exposed yourself to a lover - gave him a glimpse of your inner soul without the fear he'll walk away? One year ago? Five years ago? Ever?"

She tried to turn away from the raw words whispered

against her ear, but he grasped her chin between his fingers. "I want to know who you are. Use your mask to hide your face and feel safe, but give me the truth. I'm tired, too." His voice grew weary; distant. "I want to see beyond the surface just this once. We have the opportunity of a lifetime right before us, we can both be ourselves and still be safe."

She turned to meet his gaze. "And what about you, Phantom? I'm supposed to be vulnerable while you give nothing?"

"I'll answer any question you ask. Give you every fantasy you have ever wanted. Isn't that enough?"

Still, she hesitated.

"I promise I won't hurt you. Everything we do together will be for your pleasure. But there will no halfway. All or nothing."

At that moment, everything broke free within her. Her fantasy had been granted. She could explore the hidden parts of her sexuality with a man she desired. She could open herself up to this person in all the ways she had hidden over the years. Another man would finally know who she was – her body and soul. After being locked away in emotional isolation for her whole life – Ciro Demitris had offered the key to freedom.

But, God, what a price.

An icy chill raced down her spine and threw her into a panic. The taunting voices of her parents took hold – warning her to step back before it was too late. The image of her own night of personal heartbreak passed before her eyes. She would get hurt. He could use her and laugh and she would be alone again, except this time without pride and steeped in humiliation. What if she showed him everything she was and it wasn't enough? What if he played a cruel game for his amusement? He would strip both her body and soul bare, and she'd be helpless against him.

The thoughts tangled in her mind like a whirling cyclone.

Then, Hailey realized she had nothing more to lose.

She was already alone and afraid to venture into any intimate relationships. This was her time to take a chance and believe in herself. She was so tired of being fearful of every twist and turn life threw out. She had done everything her parents had asked; she had been a good girl. But tonight was an opportunity to let her body fly; to selfishly take pleasure and revel in it. She could not walk away from this gift thrown at her feet.

"I need your answer. Will you give yourself to me until the masquerade is over?"

His hips continued the slow rocking, and liquid heat pulsed between her legs. She arched backward in a blatant invitation, and gave him her answer.

"Yes. I'll do what you ask."

His breath hissed behind her. Without words, he took her hand and led her up to the room she had found him in. He shut the heavily carved door and stared at her in the sudden silence.

Haily faced him, ready for wherever the night took her.

CHAPTER THREE

GOD, she was stunning.

Theodore stared as she stood in the center of the room, her shimmering blue dress falling to the floor, fiery red waves of hair spilling down her back. Her long white fingers clenched and unclenched in both anticipation and fear. Finally, he'd be able to satisfy this primal craving to claim her. She was his for the next three nights and would obey every command. The bargain made not only gave him her body, but her inner soul.

It was more than he'd ever expected.

"Do you want me to undress?"

A smile touched his lips at her faintly trembling voice. "I'd like to ask you a few questions first. When was the last time you had a man fuck you?"

She jerked back at the crude word, but Theo caught the gleam of excitement she couldn't seem to hide. Yes. She liked dirty talk, but was afraid to indulge.

"It's been a few years," she said.

He lifted an eyebrow in surprise, then took a few graceful steps toward her. "Your choice?"

"Yes."

"Why?"

"No reason." His lips tightened in disapproval. Hailey hesitated, then seemed to remember the terms of her bargain. Her words were reluctant. "My parent's believed sex was wrong. I grew up on the notion that the act was something behind closed doors, something to be ashamed of."

"Go on," he urged, taking the time to light a cigarette. Sometimes, he loved to indulge in the vice he'd quit years ago, and this weekend was all about chasing pleasure. He was patient as she gathered her thoughts.

"I heard stories from others, stories of wild encounters that left women helpless for more. I was scared. I never wanted to lose any control over my life, afraid I'd become a man's play toy and then be left behind. I decided it would be easier to ignore sex and go after the things that were safe."

He took a deep pull on the cigarette and blew out the smoke in a lazy circle. "Do you ever pleasure yourself?"

A blush stained her cheeks when she thought of the torturous nights and her dreams. "No."

"But you'll leave these reservations behind for our bargain?"

She nodded. "If you command me to."

He gave a slow smile. Pink flushed her cheeks, and he realized there was a lot he hadn't known about Hailey. Particularly that she may have some submissive tendencies that could be teased out. He intended to take his time offering up various sexual scenarios so he knew what turned her on. He'd played with taking a dominant role in the bedroom before, but always craved more. Maybe this was as much his opportunity as hers. "Good. I admire control in a woman. The proper control can extend sexual pleasure for hours on end. Take your dress off."

Her fingers fumbled slightly on the back zipper. The tab slid down and the hiss cut through the silence. The material pooled at her feet. She wore a black garter belt and sheer black stockings with heels. A black lacy bra molded her breasts. Her breathing became heavier, but she managed to stand quietly before him. The smoke drifted through the room and mixed with the scent of her arousal. God, he couldn't wait to taste her. "Let's go over the rules."

She blinked but remained still.

"Keep your gaze on me at all times. Listen to what I ask. If anything I do is too much, or you want me to stop, say red."

"Why not no?"

"Because you may say no out loud but still crave me to continue. To push your barriers. It may excite you to know I'm not listening when you say no. That way, I know red means we stop immediately. Or you can ask me to slow down. Do you feel comfortable with that?"

She nodded.

"Good. When you hear the bell signaling the end of the party, you'll put your clothes back on and leave without another word. I'll meet you back here tomorrow night. Agreed?"

"Yes." She barely whispered the word.

"Take off your bra. I want to look at you." She unclasped the garment and dropped it on the floor. Her white breasts were heavy and ripe, tipped with pale pink nipples. Minutes ticked by as he drank his fill. A delicate flush washed over her body, almost as if she felt his hot gaze on her like a touch. "You were made to have a man touch you. Take your hands and caress yourself. That's right, feel the pointed tips of your nipples. Now imagine my own hands on you, my tongue licking at them, biting them. I would spend a long time just working your breasts, Hailey, refusing to touch any other part of your body. Now slide your underwear down and leave your garter and stockings on."

. . .

HE WATCHED HER CHEST RISE AND FALL IN TORTURED breathing. Caribbean blue eyes blazed at him, a mixture of shame, anger, and wanting, but she never took her gaze from his. The panties

slid down her legs. Fiery red curls beckoned him from across the room, and his cock throbbed to thrust inside her tight, wet heat. He stroked himself lazily as he watched her, enjoying the anticipation of what was to come like fine wine.

"You're so fucking perfect. I want to show what you've been missing by not exploring your own body." He loved the struggle on her face—the obvious need for more and reluctance to be exposed. "Slide your hand down your belly. That's right. Place your palm between your legs. Do you feel the heat?"

Her eyes half closed, obviously fighting herself. "Yes."

"Are you wet?"

She shuddered but remained in control, not moving. "Yes."

"Good. Let's test this will power, shall we?" He studied the graceful curve of her neck, the slight color on her cheeks. Her lower lip trembled, as if hating to give up her control but determined to stick to the bargain.

Theo softened his tone. He knew she was afraid and wanted to calm her. "You remind me of one of the paintings on the wall, with your red hair and lush body. I need to see more of you,

baby. You belong to me for the next three nights, and I intend on enjoying every inch of you. Part your legs."

She stiffened. He waited. Then she widened her stance.

Theodore sucked in his breath at the sight of her delicate pink lips, slick with moisture. He ground out his cigarette and forced himself to stay where he was until he gained control. God, how he wanted to stick his tongue up her wetness and taste her. Spread her legs wider and thrust into her clingy heat until her screams echoed in his ears. He laughed low with pleasure. And he would. But not tonight. Tonight was about foreplay, and he intended to enjoy the torture. He'd waited over a year for her; one more night would only heighten the climax.

Slowly, he closed the distance between them. Like a predator in flight, he circled around and allowed the folds of his cape brush against her naked buttocks. Hailey shuddered, desperate to keep her hunger in check.

Yes. Tonight, there was one lesson to be learned.

Tonight was about teaching her to surrender.

He stood behind her, placing both palms on her shoulders. Breathed in the scent of vanilla and coconut; breathed in the heady scent of female arousal. He let his

fingers slide through the thick strands of hair that fell to her curvy ass. With slow, easy motions, he continued the soothing ritual until he sensed her muscles begin to relax.

Then he cupped a fistful of the silky fire and used the ends like a paintbrush over her body, as if preparing a canvass. With quick, teasing strokes, he touched her nipples,

then moved away. Caressed the side of her breasts. Traced her cleavage. Tickled the sensitive underside of her neck. When he finally let her hair drop, he placed both hands underneath the curve of her naked breasts.

"There are times for control, and times for surrender. Your stubbornness has become your prison. Do you remember how good it feels to have a man's hands over you?"

Slow, barely-there touches urged her to lean in to his caress. He deliberately avoided her nipples and followed the path he'd traced before, using his fingers instead of her hair. Cupping the heavy weight, Theo squeezed lightly, testing the pressure, teasing a moan from her throat.

Her head slipped back to allow him more access. "That's it, baby girl. Let go and let me touch you any way I want—let me show you what you've been missing."

Hailey was losing her mind.

Her nipples grew taut and swollen, aching for more. Her heart thundered like a pack of thoroughbreds, and a sluggish, honeyed warmth pooled in the pit of her stomach, throbbed between her thighs, and made her knees grow weak. Her lids slid closed as she allowed herself to sink into the sensation. Long, tapered fingers touched her breasts, then gently plucked at her nipples, circling round and round as he urged her arousal to climb higher. She craved his tongue on the hard tips of her breasts, craved his fingers plunging inside her dampening heat.

Frustration built but he seemed content to let her body quiver in need.

Warm hands slid down her stomach, explored her belly button, the crease of her thigh, the curve of her hips. They stroked over her buttocks as his foot kicked her legs further apart for his exploration. Seething tendrils of sensation nipped at her control and her entire world narrowed to this one man and the need for more of him. For years, she'd been able to fight her desires, but tonight, as she felt his hot gaze on the private part of her, the wildness was unleashed.

His fingers separated the cheeks of her buttocks and slipped between them. A rush of wetness met him, and Hailey bit down on her lower lip to keep from crying out. Still, he didn't stop there, didn't allow her a moment of sanity, but pushed her further as he whispered in her ear the things he would do to her, with his tongue and lips and teeth and cock. The cool folds of his cloak swirled around her open legs until he stood before her; his gleaming eyes taunting the control she had built for herself. Never pulling his gaze from hers, he knelt, dragging his palms from her buttocks to the V between her legs. With gentle motions, he parted her swollen lips and exposed her completely.

"What do you want?"

She shook her head hard, as if to deny her own wanting. "Oh, please," she gasped. "I need..."

"Not yet. You're not ready enough."

A choked sob rose from her throat. Every part of her throbbed, and she let herself beg as her hips rocked forward in a demanding motion. He soothed her with his voice, but his touch stoked the fire, as his index finger slid over the swollen nub just once, then stretched inside of her, the tight channel making way for him as a rush of wetness met his entry.

Hailey knew she had never wanted anyone as badly as she wanted him in that moment, and within the loss of control came a surrender; an acceptance of her female sexuality she had never felt peace with.

Theodore was overcome by the need to possess her completely. The fantasies he had spun over the past year faded away, replaced by the reality of her sheer beauty and honesty. He knew then it was not only Hailey being taught a lesson in control. He ached to end the masquerade right now and make love to her without his mask. Instead, he pressed his face to her stomach until the impulse passed.

He murmured against the smooth skin of her belly; breathed in the musky scent of her as he removed his finger and let her settle back. Her entire body pulsed like an instrument about to be played, and within himself he felt stretched to the limit of control. Her blue eyes were wild; drugged. She gasped for breath, her nipples hard little points straining for his mouth, her clitoris so swollen only the tip of his tongue could make her come.

He couldn't remember another time he had wanted a woman more; couldn't remember when he'd reveled in such an abandoned response from just his touch. Halfway tempted to rip off his clothes and take her right now, he hesitated a moment.

A bell rang out.

Silence filled the room. A moan escaped her lips.

"You may put your clothes on." He paused. "We'll meet again tomorrow."

Hailey blinked at him in confusion. Her body shook with the need to orgasm. He watched as she opened her mouth to protest and ask him to finish. God knows, if he would've indulged both of them since he was at the edge. But she managed to reclaim control, as if realizing what she'd agreed to. She pulled her clothes back on and dressed without a word. Then she walked past him and out the door.

She followed everyone through the massive doorway and waited her turn to board the ferry. The damp, musky scent of her arousal rose to her nostrils. The other guests bumped against her as they obeyed the rules of the party. At dawn, every guest was escorted back to their various hotels. No one was allowed to return until the following night.

Hailey felt eyes upon her as she was about to step off the dock. As she settled down in the boat, she looked up and directed her gaze to the second-floor balcony off the right corner of the mansion.

A masked figure was barely visible, but she caught a glimmer of white which gleamed from the distance. The shadows closed around him and fought to reclaim its territory. When the ferry chugged through the calm waters, the figure turned and disappeared from the balcony, and Hailey wondered briefly if the whole night had only been an illusion.

But as she sat on the ferry and started to her hotel, she realized she had been flung over the edge of her sexuality. There was no going back. The thoughts of what her Phantom was going to do to her burned through her body with shame and hard-edged desire.

There would no sleep tonight.

Only anticipation for tomorrow.

CHAPTER FOUR

"GOOD EVENING."

Hailey stepped into the room and shut the door behind her. Her palms dampened with nervous perspiration. Her stomach slid and rolled like she was on a roller-coaster. The worst part was knowing the sensations were caused by excitement—not fear. She forced herself to return his greeting. "Good evening, Phantom."

He wore the black cloak. His mask tonight was smaller, still blinding white, but of a smoother material that fit snugly over his eyes and nose, but left more of his mouth free. His lips were full and perfectly sculpted, with a savage curl to the lower one that told her he could be cruel when he chose. The diamond in his left ear flashed as he turned his head. "Did you dream about me, Hailey?"

"Yes."

He walked towards her then, with a slow, masculine grace. Dark blue eyes gleamed with sexual appreciation as he took in her figure. The long tight sheath shimmered with gold sparkles, emphasizing the curve of her hips and the thrust of her breasts. "I'm glad," he said softly. "Will you walk with me?"

She drew back in surprise, then nodded. "Of course."

He led her through the party and out to the garden. The sweet scents of citrus and wild flowers saturated the air with a potency that made her feel slightly drunk. Hailey maneuvered her way over the cobblestones and when she stumbled, he reached for her hand. All five fingers interlaced with hers in a union that staked his claim. She expected a rush of intimidation. Instead, she experienced excitement.

He allowed the silence of the night to soothe and relax her. The faint sounds of Frank Sinatra's Summer Wind stroked her ears as he stopped at a stone bench hidden within the lush tangle of trees and flowers. She sat beside him. He turned her hand over and his thumb began to press and massage the sensitive skin of her palm. An involuntary sigh whispered from her lips.

He smiled. "Where do you live?"

"New York, born and bred."

"And what do you love about New York?"

She gave a chuckle. "Never ask that to a native. We love a good bagel, good baseball, and a good argument."

"So, you never wanted to leave?"

The memory teased the fringes of her mind and brought a touch of sadness. Almost as if he felt the change in her, his touch moved to each of her fingers, rubbing, pressing, soothing from the base to the fingertip. She opened her mouth to make a lighthearted remark and move on, but then she remembered her promise. Hailey took a deep breath and started talking.

"I almost left once. After my parents died, I found myself wanting to experience a different life. One of my own making. I had no other relatives so I was alone. The crowds I was so accustomed to made me even more lonely. I almost packed everything up and moved down South, but then I remembered an old friend of my father who worked in Manhattan. I decided to look him up."

"You didn't want to run away. You were strong enough to try and find who you are in the same place where you lost yourself."

His statement made her head swing around to face him. The words touched something deep within her. "Yes. That's exactly what I wanted."

"Did you father's friend help you?"

She nodded. "He was kind. He worked for a small computer firm and got me a job. I took the opportunity to learn everything about the business and made my way to manager. Now I have security. Money. Safety."

"Do you have everything you were looking for?"

Hailey thought of the long nights alone, staring out at the city chaos and longing to be one of them. She thought of Theodore, her best friend, who she used to protect herself from the unknown. "No," she said softly. "But I'm still trying."

His thumb pressed into the pulse at her wrist and felt the slow steady beat of her heart. Then he trailed his fingers up and down her arm, brushing the sensitive area behind her elbow. Comfort blended with sensuality and caused an inner battle within. His voice spun an intimacy of longtime friends. His touch spun a web of raw edged desire and hunger.

"Sometimes it's easier to blame your past. Parents seem to have this control over children. And when they're gone, we realize there are no more obstacles to stop us from what we really want." He paused. "What did your parents keep you from?"

She sighed into the night and let the words spill from her lips. "Everything. Life. My mother got pregnant young and my father was forced to marry her. They never let me forget I was a mistake so I was raised that sex was wrong. Especially after they found religion." She shook her head at the memories. "My weekends were spent in church and confession. I was never able to date, or go to parties, or be a normal kid. I always dreamed of making my own choices. I wanted freedom so desperately, but when I didn't have my parents anymore, nothing made sense."

"You have to find your own sense."

Something changed in the air. She sucked in her breath as they both felt the comfort twist to desire, and his fingers tightened around her arm. Their brief talk had smashed all the barriers she erected last night, and the trembling began deep in the pit of her belly as she realized tonight her Phantom would stake his claim.

"I want to ask you a question," he said softly. "Were you excited when you thought of what we had done in that room?" He accepted her nod as an answer. "And did you pleasure yourself in your bed last night?"

Her voice came out in a whisper. "No."

His fingers reached out to touch her face. Slowly traced around the gold mask she wore. His thumb roughly pressed over her mouth, parted her lips, and dragged his flesh across her lower teeth. She tasted his skin and wanted more. He lowered his head. His warm breath caressed her as he continued speaking. "Before I take you back upstairs, I want truth. What stops you from taking your own pleasure? I can't believe you'd turn away from your own sexuality for all these years. Your parents are gone, Hailey. What else are you afraid of?"

She didn't want to answer, but his fingers gently stroked her cheek, her hair, her jawline. She was vulnerable to him when he was kind, and the knowledge gleamed in his eyes, reminding her at the end of the masquerade he would have more of her than any other man.

She had never spoken of that night to anyone. But now, with her face safely hidden, she decided to tell the truth. "My parents didn't allow me to go away to school, so I went to the local community college and lived at home. I was nineteen when I met him. He was in my Biology class. I thought he was beautiful. Blonde hair, green eyes, and a smile that made me melt. I'd never strayed from my parent's rules, but that weekend when he asked me out, I couldn't say no."

She took a deep breath and continued. "I lied to my mother and snuck out to meet him. We went to one of those college parties I heard so much about. I remember the drinking, and the drugs, and the wild sex going on in the rooms. I was overwhelmed but excited. I felt ready to take a chance and finally be a normal teenager."

He remained silent, his touch on her cheek supportive.

"After a few drinks, he took me into one of the rooms. We just talked at first, then started kissing. I never felt like that before. All geared up and wanting something I was so afraid of. But then he started moving faster, and too soon his clothes were off, and I was confused. I just wanted to kiss, but he kept going and…"

Hailey trailed off. Raised her chin. Then forced the words out. "We had sex. I didn't want to, but didn't really remember fighting him. Things happened so fast and it was over and I felt…. used. He put on his pants and thanked me for the good time. Then left the room.

"I heard laughter from outside and knew he was telling his friends how he got laid. I ran all the way home and never saw him again."

Ciro's hand was gentle as he stroked her hair. There was a protective gleam in his eyes she found comforting. "So, your first experience confirmed what your parents had been telling you all along."

She gave a bitter laugh. "Yes. I was afraid to go back and run into him. I was afraid I would be pregnant and end up exactly like my mother. That's when I decided they were right. Sex took away control, and I promised myself I would never feel like that again."

The emotions warred inside of her, until every secret fear she battled spilled helplessly from her lips. "Don't you see?"

she whispered. "I don't want any man to have that power over me. At least I'll be safe."

"You'll be alone."

"But safe," she repeated fiercely.

Warm hands cupped her cheeks. His lips stopped inches from hers. "Turning away from your womanhood is giving you a false sense of control. You let that asshole rapist win. You've let your parents win. Use me and fight back, Hailey." His words dripped over her like hot caramel. His eyes dared her to meet his lips halfway. "You're a beautiful, sexual woman who had a horrible experience. I can show you how to take your pleasure from a man without feeling shame. When I'm done with you, you'll beg for more. And you'll feel empowered—not degraded. Do you want me?"

Her voice broke. "Yes."

"Come with me."

He led her back through the garden, up the stairs, into the room they shared the night

before. Shut the door. Then faced her. "Do you want me?" he asked again.

The dam broke open. Hailey stumbled two steps and reached for him, standing on tiptoes to meet his lips. She repeated her answer with a deep sense of hunger, her rush of breath mingling with his. "Yes."

"Kiss me."

His lips took hers, his tongue sliding with slow, deep strokes to engage in a sensual game of plunge and retreat. He tasted of smoke and fine brandy and hot male wanting. His tongue tangled around hers, his lips closing in a gentle suction as he took her fully into his mouth. They drank of each other with greed. His teeth sank into the plump lower lip and bit down carefully. The hot wave of sensation seized her between her legs. A sob caught in her throat. She wanted him to take her like an animal, wanted to open herself up to every fantasy he ever had, and as if he knew what she was thinking, he drew back slightly and lowered the zipper of the gold sheath.

The fabric pooled around her feet. She wore nothing underneath.

Theo stared at her, hot eyes devouring every inch of her skin. Plump white breasts were swollen, tipped by tight pink nipples. The smooth skin of her belly trembled slightly, sloping into a mass of fiery red curls that hid her lips from him. Cherry red toenails curled into the burgundy carpeting in anticipation of what was to come.

Theodore swore softly under his breath. All the questions had been suddenly answered. He fought the need to rip off his mask and take her in his arms for comfort. He fought the rage that urged him to find the man who had hurt her and make him pay. But he did none of that. He knew this was a chance to give her something back – something that had been taken from her too

young. And he knew in that moment he had never loved anyone as much as he loved Hailey Ashton.

He wanted to give her an ecstasy she had never experienced before. He wanted to free her of demons and watch her smile. He wanted to possess every part of her body and soul – even if she met his unmasked face at the end and turned away. This woman shared deep truths about herself. He respected her strength, and her honesty, and swore by the time she walked away, she would never deny her sexuality again.

Tonight, he would claim her like no other man had before.

CHAPTER FIVE

CIRO LED her over to the window and positioned her in front of him. The sleek folds of his cloak caressed her naked buttocks and thighs. She felt his hard cock press against her, and she gripped the edge of the windowsill as the waves of heat sliced through her body. Her gaze blindly sought out the lights in the distance. The balmy night air washed over her skin, and the sounds of the party rose upward in waves of music and laughter and moans of satisfaction. In every room tonight, another sexual game was being played out, and Hailey felt the sheer excitement of being one of them, reveling in her nakedness and in the man who was about to take her.

"Close your eyes," he demanded in a low, gravelly tone. "I want you to feel everything I do to you. You're not allowed to turn around or to touch me. Do you understand?"

"Yes."

Large hands slipped around her waist and skated upward to cup her heavy breasts. His thumbs rubbed over her nipples, and the sensitive peaks tingled, pearling into hard points. One foot nudged her legs apart, widening her stance, so she was open to him. He spoke into her ear. His teeth pulled at the lobe as his tongue darted around the sensitive shell in hot, quick licks.

"I'm going to do everything to you tonight. I'm going to make you beg and plead and cry for me before I give you what you want." Every part of her body was being touched, tasted, his tongue in her ear, his fingers on her breasts, his hard cock rubbing against her buttocks in a teasing motion that made a moan spill from her lips. His palm slid down her belly and cupped the junction of red curls. He separated her plump lips slowly, and she felt the rush of air against her hard, throbbing clitoris in a maddening caress. His thumb caressed the miniature bud with a slow, steady rhythm, then stopped when her hips bucked upward against his hand in a plea for release. His teeth bit her neck, sucked hard, and one finger slid between her lips and entered her, his flesh instantly soaked with her wetness. She felt the excitement within her build, craving an orgasm, but every time he brought her right to the edge he stopped, until she begged him in unconscious broken pleas.

Pleasure. Pain. Wanting. Need.

"I won't let you come until I'm inside of you, baby. Not until you scream at the top of your lungs for me to take you."

Suddenly, both hands slipped down her body and pried her legs further apart. While one thumb teased her pulsing bud, he used his other hand to plunge three fingers at once into her, moving in and out with a ferocious pace until she did as she asked, screaming wildly for her take her, and then he bent her forward and rammed his cock into her tight, clinging heat.

She climaxed immediately. Multiple waves of ecstasy washed over her, through her. Her breasts swayed freely in the night breeze. Her head arched upward as her hips rocked against the grinding of his cock, invading every inch of her body. He pumped himself in her over and over, not letting her first orgasm pass until another one took hold, and then she sobbed for the pleasure to stop it was too much, but he kept going on and on. His dick slid all the way out before pounding back, so deep inside she felt her G-spot tickled and teased until she came again. Then he let himself go, and his come exploded deep inside of her, washing upward and then trickling down her open thighs. Hailey sobbed with the intensity of release. He held and stroked her with comfort until she quieted. He closed the window and guided her over to the bed.

Like a child, he laid her upon the burgundy satin sheets, and stripped off his own cloak to rest beside her. Silence bathed the room. She listened to his deep breathing, her head on his chest, his arms pulling her tight against him.

She finally felt able to speak. "That wasn't fair."

A deep chuckle rumbled through his chest. "You had multiple orgasms. How wasn't that fair?"

She lifted her head to look at him. His blue eyes gleamed behind the white mask. "I didn't get to look at you. Touch you. Am I going to get a shot at torturing you?"

The distant air he normally exuded faded away. His hands played with her long red curls and his face softened with humor. "I don't think that was in the agreement."

"Maybe we need an amendment."

"Ah, but then you wouldn't get the final goal. I get your full cooperation for four nights. Then at the end you can make your own decision."

He was holding back. Hailey wondered why she felt so sad. She'd agreed to the terms and knew this game was only about sex. It was important to keep her own distance, even though she craved more knowledge about the man beside her.

As Ciro Demitris.

Not the Phantom.

She spoke hesitantly. "You said you believe people only show the surface. Do you know why?"

The corner of his lips twitched slightly. "Do I get a guess or do you just tell me the answer?"

"Wise ass," she muttered.

He laughed, and pulled her back into his embrace when she would have grouchily turned away. "Tell me."

"It's so much easier to give people what they expect. Do you remember what it was like to be a child, Phantom?"

"Barely."

"I do. I remember I used to run everywhere because I was so excited to see what part of life came next. Then my mother told me it wasn't ladylike to run. People expected me to behave

a certain way, and I got a reward when I was quiet and dignified. So, I became what they wanted."

He stroked her hair back from her forehead. His voice was thoughtful. "Do you miss running?"

She gave a deep sigh. "I miss the other part."

"What part?"

"Wanting to see what happens next. After a while, it became so much easier to walk. There was nothing exciting to run for."

They were silent for a while, but his hands soothed and stroked. His body heat comforted and Hailey relaxed deeper into the smooth, cool sheets. "Once you stopped running, what else gave you pleasure? Do you have anything you're passionate about in life?"

The faint sounds of the orchestra drifted through the window. The flickering of the candle lent an air of intimacy as she spoke. "I enjoy many things. Reading, movies, good food and good wine. Opera."

"La Traviata."

She rolled over to face him and laughed in delight. "Yes, my favorite. A little dramatic for a man, I always thought."

"Now who's being a chauvinist?"

She placed an impulsive kiss on his lips. "You're right."

"Have you ever been married?"

"No."

"Children?"

A twinge of sadness coursed through her. "No."

He seemed to catch her response. "Do you want children?"

"I want a dozen. But I want the whole picture, including the husband and house and happy marriage."

He reached out to touch her cheek. "Why do women always want to settle down and men always want to run away?"

Hailey smiled. "I don't believe that. I think everyone wants to meet their true soul-mate. Once that happens, a person makes a choice to either take a chance or stay safe. Women sometimes settle for somebody less than a true love because they're afraid no one else will come along. And men just get scared of what will happen if they do meet their true love."

"Not fear, Hailey. Maybe some men realize the real thing isn't out there."

She let his words simmer for a moment before answering. "Do you do this often, Phantom?" she asked. "Bargain with a woman for everything, then walk away?"

He stiffened beneath her. "No."

"Why did you?"

"Maybe I was tired of running myself." She opened her mouth to respond, but he continued, his words growing fierce. "You say you want a husband and children. A soul-mate. You may want these things but they come at a price, Hailey. Are you willing to lose this control and take a chance? Or is it still easier to just live in the fantasy?"

She wondered at his anger, but he suddenly rolled over and pinned her beneath him. Within moments, his face cleared. The humor was back. "Why do I feel we suddenly switched roles? Are you using my temporary weakness to plunder my secrets?"

Her eyes widened. "I don't think your weakness was all that temporary." His erection pressed with demand against her inner thigh. "I thought, I thought men needed a little bit more, er, time."

He grinned wickedly. "You were lied to. Your education about a man's true abilities has just begun. But first I want you to drink something for me."

He left the bed and brought back a glass of sparkling white liquid in a heavily cut glass. She looked at him questioningly.

"It's a slight aphrodisiac," he explained. "Quite harmless. The drink will heighten your senses and lengthen your pleasure."

She nodded and took a sip. The sharp, fruity essence washed over her tongue. Her lips pursed with enjoyment over the taste, then he took the glass from her. "Here, let me," he murmured. He filled his mouth with the liquid, leaned over, and slowly let the spiked wine trickle from his lips into her mouth. The warm liquid slid down her throat in a sensual caress, and she felt her body quicken again. He put the glass on the bedside table, then rose from the bed again.

Hailey watched him with heavily lidded eyes, enjoying his nakedness. He moved with a muscled grace uncommon to men, his chest and shoulders broad, his buttocks firm, his legs long and lean. His dick was full and thick. Her mouth watered to taste him. Whipcord strength rippled from every carved muscle as he made his way through the room. When he returned to the bed, he had a corded silk rope, and two vials of oil. Already the effect of the wine coursed through her. The cool satin sheets slid over her naked skin. She made a noise low in her throat as she stretched out on the bed. Her sex throbbed with slow, heavy pulses and her flesh became hot as she watched him approach.

He knelt between her thighs. She moaned and opened her legs, inviting him to take her again. She imagined what she looked like; spread open; pussy lips flushed pink and gleaming with wetness. The image made her squirm in growing hunger. "Phantom," she whispered urgently.

Theo watched as a sharp longing cut through him. Damnit, he wanted her to say his own name, wanted her to know this was him to give her such intense pleasure. Then he pushed the thought away and concentrated on the moment. For now, she belonged to him, and he intended to enjoy their time together. He knew she was already feeling the effect of the wine, and anticipation shot through him at having her at his will. "What do you want, sweetness?" he asked.

"I want you to take me again. I want you deep and hard inside me."

"I intend to. But not yet. I have some other plans." He took the rope and gently tied both of her wrists to the bedpost, so her arms were tightly bound above her head. Her breasts arched upward in a gift he intended to enjoy.

"What are you doing?"

He smiled at her sultry tone. "I want to enjoy every inch of your body, Hailey, in every way possible. I intend to taste you and play with you a little more."

She tugged at the silken ropes, and he knew her absolute helplessness only added to her desire. He reached over and uncapped a small vial of oil. The heady scents of incense and herbs rose in the air. Slowly, he poured the oil onto his fingers. Then he coated the tips of both nipples with careful precision, avoiding the heavy weight of her breasts. When each point gleamed, he placed a dab on the swell of her belly right above her pubic hair. Then his knees widened her legs further apart. He took the vial and tipped it right above her clitoris,

watching the golden liquid coat the tiny throbbing member and slide over her pink lips.

She moaned and tugged at her restraints.

"The oil will make your body even more sensitive. You should get a tight, tingling feeling. The special herbs will bring a focus to certain parts."

"I'm so hot." Her head tossed back and forth against the pillow. "Everything feels so strange. I'm floating, but my body is on fire. God, what are you doing to me?"

"I'm going to fuck you. Make you come. Make you beg." God, his words made dampness trickle down her inner thighs. She liked his dirty talk. Liked being tied up and open for his pleasure. Theo imagined her back in the real world, allowing him to do this in her own bedroom while she screamed his name. Need squeezed his muscles but Theo knew it wasn't time. At the end of this experiment, they would both make their choices. For now, nothing mattered except the moment.

His mouth settled over one breast, and his tongue slowly licked at the strawberry pink tip which gleamed wetly with oil. Her breasts swelled beneath his lips, but he kept the pace slow and easy, knowing she'd be wild by the time he thrust inside her. His teeth scraped against her nipple, then he took the whole tip in his mouth and sucked hard. She tugged at her restraints in an urge to grab him, as he palmed her other breast, then moved his mouth to its twin to continue the torture. He licked and sucked for long, long minutes, until her engorged nipples were so sensitive, even the slight rush of his breath against her made her cry out. Still, he continued the torture, his thumb lazily circling her gorgeous breasts, watching every flicker of emotion gleaming in those blue eyes. His tongue flicked hard at the tight buds. Grasped them with his fingers.

And twisted.

She bucked under the sudden pain, but Theo relished the rush of wetness from her sweet pussy. "You like that baby?"

"I don't know."

He gave a wicked chuckle. His fingers pushed inside her sopping channel. Her walls gripped him in greed. "Oh, yeah, you loved it. What more can I do to you?"

"Phantom. Please!"

"Tell me everything you feel."

He loved watching her embrace every one of her needs, finally free from the restraints she locked herself in during the day. "I'm burning. Everything is tight and tingly but it hurts down there. I need—"

"Say it. Your pretty little clit needs my tongue. Your sweet pussy needs my dick."

"Yes," she whispered, her body shaking.

He nipped at her belly button. Ran his tongue along the path of her fiery curls covering her mound. Then paused, staring up her naked body, smiling slowly. "Say it, Hailey. Tell me all the dirty things you want me to do to you."

Low, animal noises rose from her throat. Theo reveled in the moment she broke, desperate for release. She yanked at her restraints with a vicious urgency. "Put your mouth on my pussy. Suck my clit and make me come. I need you!"

"That's my good girl."

Satisfaction surged. Theo pushed her knees up and dragged them apart so she was open to his mouth. He blew gently on the red curls, parting them so her throbbing wet lips were exposed. Her head tossed back and forth on the pillow. His mouth dipped and he feasted on her, hungry for the sweet, spicy taste of her, His tongue swiped once. Twice.

She came hard, screaming, grinding against his open mouth with her own demand. He let her ride out the orgasm, his fingers gripping her hips.

"Yes, baby, that's it. Come all over my face like the good, dirty girl you are."

She sobbed as another mini convulsion shook through her.

Theo chuckled with satisfaction, then lowered his head

once again. This time his tongue licked gently at her throbbing clit, bringing her back up. Sliding in and out in lazy motions, his fingers curled and pushed inside her, keeping up a steady rhythm she couldn't fight. "You're so beautiful," he said, pressing kisses to her pussy. "Like a flower opening to the sun, you taste like moist rose petals. What do you want me to do to you? Tell me."

Her hips pushed for more as every muscle clenched. His teeth scraped across the sensitive bud and his tongue soothed the sting. "There's no shyness here, baby. I need to hear your sweet voice begging."

"Oh, God. Please fuck me, Phantom. Make me come again."

He sucked hard on her clit, taking her to the razor edge. But Theo couldn't control himself anymore, so with one swift movement he brought himself to his knees, spreading her legs wide.

Raw possessiveness surged through him as he studied the woman he loved.

Naked. Open. Trembling with need for him to mess her up and fuck her until she had nothing left to give.

Griping her hips to yank her up high, he pushed his dick inside her in one swift motion.

A gasp escaped her swollen lips. Her fingers wrapped around the ropes, holding tight.

"Hang on, sweetness."

Theo took her hard, driving his cock deep, until it was buried to the hilt in her wet, clinging flesh. He slid easily in and out, making sure to scrape against her clit, using the slick oil to make the motions more intense. And then she was squeezing his cock and coming around him. He watched with satisfaction as she rode out her orgasm, and then he let himself go. His balls tightened and he came hard, hips jerking, the brutal pleasure shocking his body.

Finally, he collapsed on top of her. Her spread legs

cradled him, their juices sticky and warm over her body. He untied the ropes, rubbing her arms and fingers to make sure she hadn't gone numb. When he finished, Hailey turned into his arms as if she belonged there. Her fingers buried into his hair. He closed his eyes halfway, realizing this game was more dangerous than he'd ever intended.

Theo savored the moment. She'd given everything he dreamed of.

It had only been to the wrong person.

The bell rang.

He lifted his head. Their gazes locked. A question burned between them, unanswered, unspoken. His chest hurt as he rose from the bed and watched her get dressed, then slipped on his cloak. Seconds slipped by but he made no other move toward her. It was too much. Theo was afraid she'd know the truth if he spoke, and then both their fantasies would be over.

He wasn't ready to let her go yet.

Maybe she'd admit the same. Maybe she sensed it was him behind the mask. Maybe she was ready to walk into the daytime with him by her side, no longer needing a made-up Phantom to make her feel wanted.

Hailey turned and ducked her head. Her voice was husky when she finally spoke.

"Good night, Phantom."

His heart shattered. He embraced the ice forming inside him, his mouth tightening in a firm line as he stared back at her.

"Good night."

She waited. One moment. Two.

Then left.

SOMETHING HAD CHANGED.

As she rode the ferry home, Hailey shivered in the wind, even though it was another balmy evening. When Ciro released the ropes, fierce waves of protective need rose inside her, and she'd only wanted to hold him. This strong, sexy billionaire had exuded a vulnerability that shook her.

Somehow, a connection had been formed that went beyond the physical. He reached a part of her that she'd locked up for years, but her surrender didn't make her feel weak.

Instead, a powerful strength in her newfound sexuality pounded in her veins. Though she'd been tied up and helpless, her Phantom made her surrender seem sexy.

Hailey had no idea sex could be like that. The previous assault pushed her to distrust her instincts. Tonight, she'd been a free, confident woman who held no shame demanding pleasure.

Even as her cheeks heated from the memory, a smile curved her lips.

Within these past hours, she'd reclaimed a precious gift.

Her sexual freedom.

Throughout their encounter, even though she was the one who was supposed to give everything, she never felt alone. Messy emotions stirred like a kicked wasp nest. Why did this simple arrangement seem to be more than what either of them had agreed?

Because this felt so much bigger than just sex.

It was something more like love.

The ferry docked. She made her way back to the hotel, thinking of what tomorrow would bring.

She took a shower, enjoying the hot water pouring over her aching muscles. She dressed in her pjs and crawled onto the mattress. The heavy four poster bed was quite comfortable, but her mind was focused on other bedrooms, ones with satin sheets and masked Phantoms.

Though she was exhausted, Hailey tossed and turned.

Where had the idea of love come from anyway? Logically, she understood her body had finally been freed from bondage, and she was a little vulnerable. She'd confessed something in her past that no one had ever known, not even Theodore. Perhaps, almost like a therapist, she developed an attachment for the man who helped her.

At least, Hailey knew one thing. The years of denying her sexuality were over. She would move forward and embrace her physical desires, refusing to be shamed by them. Ciro Demitris had taught her that. Gratitude washed through her.

The phone rang.

She jumped and glanced at the name. Her heart leapt. "Hello?"

"Hailey?"

She smiled when she heard Theodore's voice. "I'm fine."

A sigh of relief echoed in her ear. "Good. I was a little worried. How's the party?"

"Amazing. The island is beautiful, and the mansion is out of a movie. Way out of my normal league."

"Doubt it. You were born for luxury. And a man who can spoil you."

Goose bumps broke out on her skin. There was an intimacy tangled within his words she didn't know how to analyze. "Well, I certainly don't hate it."

He gave a low laugh. "Am I going to have to ask? Or are you afraid to tell me?"

Hailey took a deep breath. "I met him. Ciro. He was dressed as the Phantom just like you said."

"Was he everything you expected?"

"Yes. Even more."

"Wow. You just met him. He must've made an impression."

The hard edge to his voice made her stiffen. "He's not what you think. He may have a lot of money, but he's lonely. I feel like we connected."

"Did you kiss him?"

She hesitated. Odd, she should feel almost guilty by telling her best friend. "Yes."

A pause. "Your knees buckled?"

Hailey laughed. "Yeah, they crumbled right beneath me. We both agreed to keep our masks on and reveal our faces the final night. But I'm scared of unmasking. What if he sees I'm just this ordinary woman beneath all the makeup and costume?"

"What if he does?"

She sighed. "I guess you're right. I've come too far to stop now. How are things on the home front?"

"The Bulls lost."

"See, you should have come with me," she teased.

"And cramp your style? Nah, someone has to get their full eight hours sleep."

"Then why are you up at 6:00am on a Saturday?" she asked knowingly.

He made a gruff noise over the phone. "I wanted to make sure you were still intact."

His voice in the dark was oddly comforting, and she thought once again how lucky she was to have a friend who cared so much about her. "Thank you, Theodore."

"For what?"

"For always being there. For putting up with my moods and making me laugh. For being my best friend."

"Man, are you in a mushy mood tonight," he grumbled. "I only called to say good night."

Hailey laughed. "My romantic hero. You always run away when I get emotional."

"Yeah, yeah. How are the overnight accommodations?"

"Fancy. He blocked a whole bunch of inns on the island for his guests. I'm staying at this little bed and breakfast with a huge four poster bed. I thought I'd need a ladder to climb up."

"Just don't break a leg getting down." He paused. "Hailey, did anything else happen between you two tonight?"

An array of erotic images flashed before her; images of the Phantom thrusting inside her, his tongue deep inside her mouth; his arms pinning her against the bed. She shuddered with the memory and opened her mouth to tell her friend everything.

Then realized she couldn't.

Theodore would never understand the dark, secret part of her who longed to be a sexual being. He supported her and kept her safe. He was sweet and kind and safe. After his heart had been broken by his lover, he had closed a part off. Hailey knew they had connected so well because she had done the same thing. Now, she wanted to be free.

But he was still trapped.

No, Theodore was better off not knowing the truth. Hailey took a deep breath and lied. "Nothing else happened."

Silence hummed over the line. When Theodore spoke his voice was tight with emotion. "I'm sorry I couldn't make you feel like that. Good night, Hailey."

"Good night."

She clicked off and stared out into the darkness. A strange ache lay heavily around her heart and she wasn't sure why. Something in her friend's voice made her miss him. Almost as if he was as lonely in the darkness as she, and wanted to feel a connection. His last words were so odd. How could he possibly know how she felt about Ciro Demitris?

Thoughts of Theodore whirled with images of her Phantom, until she closed her eyes to avoid the tangle of feelings and fell into a deep sleep.

THEODORE STARED AT THE PHONE AND FELL BACK ON THE pillows. Hands clasped behind his head, he thought of her voice and what she had shared with him tonight.

For the first time, there was no barrier between them. Clothes had fallen away, skin touched against skin, but even more powerful was her gift of self. He understood now all the moments she distanced herself from him, afraid of the past, afraid of wanting something that could burn out of control. He needed to use these last nights to imprint himself into her so deeply she could never run away again.

The masquerade had been successful so far. He made sure he stayed behind as the guests left, remaining in the same bedroom where he'd first spotted Hailey. He hired his own private boat to pick him up at the mansion a half hour past dawn, so she'd never suspect the ruse. Every last detail had been arranged, yet he still feared the final unmasking. She was falling in love with him, yet she believed he was Ciro Demitris. She was ripening before his eyes, and he was the one who had set her free. But was Hailey ready to accept the terms of a real relationship, or would she now want to be free? Would she crave to experience everything she had missed out on? Would she turn away from him to embark on affairs?

He'd set up his plan in order to claim his lady. Yet, he now realized by setting her free, he may lose her forever.

Theodore turned out the light and gazed into the dark of the room. The question burned in his mind for a long while before sleep finally claimed him.

CHAPTER SIX

THEO WATCHED her walk in the room, her step halfway hesitant as she closed the door behind her. Tonight, she wore an ebony dress that tied around the neck in a halter style, then plunged low in the front and left her back bare. Her mask was held together by vibrant feathers, making her blue eyes even more mysterious.

As she stopped before him, he didn't speak. Just looked at her. The sheer beauty of her presence made his heart pound faster. He dreamed of her last night. Their conversation haunted him, along with his troubled thoughts, and his weakness for her suddenly made him angry.

All those evenings they spent together, talking long after the sun set about their lives. She called him her friend, but never shared her past. She believed him to be safe, but when he made the slightest move to deepen the relationship, she backed away. Yet here she was before him, thinking he was a stranger. With Ciro Demitris she revealed everything – underneath her clothes and into her soul in a way she never let him in.

Theo had slipped into the role of the tycoon with an ease that surprised him. When he donned the cloak and mask, he decided to let his own secret fantasies take hold. He became dominant and demanding with his pleasure. He knew Hailey wanted intrigue and fantasy, and he'd given both to her. What he didn't realize was the emotions he used to be the Phantom were quite real. He was lonely and isolated. He longed for sexual freedom and a woman to fly in his arms. Everything he spoke to her as Demitris was the truth.

And that scared the hell out of him.

Suddenly, Theo didn't want to play the game anymore. He wanted to tell her the truth, and watch her shock when he revealed himself. He wanted to hear his own name echo through the air instead of the false Phantom.

Jealousy bit through him. His eyes narrowed with an anger he no longer wanted to hide. He spoke like he imagined Ciro would, formally dismissing her. "I'm not in the mood for elaborate games tonight. You've begun to bore me. I won't be requiring your service."

HAILEY FLINCHED. SOMETHING HAD CHANGED. A WALL shimmered around him that froze her out. She stared and searched for a sign of his true feelings, but he only walked to the dresser to take a cigarette and light it.

Hailey tightened her arms around her breasts in a protective gesture. Was this it? The end of a charade she'd believed was becoming real?

The moment she'd seen him, her body quickened, but now doubt flickered in her mind. Tonight, he wore his cruelty like his cloak, but Hailey remembered when she first walked in and their gazes locked. Anticipation gleamed within those navy-blue depths. Along with a tendril of fear. The emotion was easy to recognize; she felt the same mixture.

He smoked his cigarette with leisure, refusing to turn and

look at her. His shoulders remained stiff and unyielding. Hailey turned to go, half relieved at her dismissal, but paused with her hand on the knob. Her Phantom was not so invulnerable to the game. Somehow, feelings had begun to develop, and Hailey refused to cower before them. She had made her bargain. Truth at all costs.

She crossed the room, reached out, and lay one hand on his upper arm. The muscles jumped beneath her touch. He spun around in a whirl of black, his mouth turned down in a sneer. "Why are you still here? I said I don't desire you tonight."

His obvious anger soothed her. If he didn't care, he'd show mercy. "Then I'll wait until you do."

He muttered something under his breath. "What are you trying to prove? I'm the one who makes the rules of this game. You obey me, no matter what. And I'm choosing to dismiss you."

Hailey lifted her chin in the air. "I will obey, because we made a bargain, Phantom. But we're also supposed to tell the truth to each other. You're breaking our pact. I had no idea you were a coward."

He grabbed her arms and lifted up, yanking her against him. His warm breath struck her lips. "You dare to call me a coward? Perhaps, you don't want to hear your own truth. That I don't want you anymore. That you now bore me, and I crave another woman."

Her hands automatically clenched around the folds of his cloak as she hung on. Hailey prayed her bluff would work. "Then I call you a liar. And if you must prove something to yourself, I'll wait while you take another woman, and join you after. Because I made a promise. I want to be with you tonight, no matter what the cost."

A vicious curse cut through the air. "Damn you!"

His mouth stamped over hers. With one quick thrust, his tongue parted her lips and conquered her with dominant, hard strokes, exploring every damp, hidden crevice, claiming her for his own.

She gave it all back to him. Her fingernails dug into his shoulders as she wrapped her legs around his waist and hung on. He thrust all ten fingers into the heavy weight of her hair to hold her head still, as he took more of her, his tongue battling with hers. His taste and the male scent of him swamped her senses. He nipped at her lower lip, then drew it deep into his mouth to suck hard. When he finally pulled away, she struggled for breath.

Slowly, he allowed her to slide back down his body until her feet once again touched the floor.

"Phantom?"

He closed his eyes in defeat. Then took her gently in his arms. "I'm sorry, Hailey." She glanced up at him. Disgust carved out his features. "I wanted to hurt you."

"Why?" He remained silent. She pulled away and looked into his face. Then ran her fingers over the sculpted curve of his lower lip, his chiseled jawline, his cheekbone. "You didn't hurt me. I hear your voice and my body becomes ready instantly. I close my eyes and all I can imagine is your hands on me. I want you all the time. But tonight you seem so angry."

"I was angry at myself."

"But you're not going to tell me why."

"I've never wanted a woman as much as I want you. I've never enjoyed a woman's company as I do yours. I hate when you leave at the night's end, and I wish I could sleep with you and wake up to your smile. That's why I'm angry."

Her heart lightened and expanded like a balloon. A husky laugh escaped her lips, and she reached up to kiss him. Her lips moved over his and savored the taste of smoke, the sting of cognac, and the arousal of male hunger. Her tongue slipped inward, touching the tip of his in a teasing caress, then drank deeply of him. When she finally raised her head, she couldn't hide her delight.

"Let me give you some advice. When a woman hears words like that from her lover, it means everything. I'm inexperienced, so to know I made such an impression fills me up." She paused. "I feel the same way about you."

"We shouldn't complicate matters." His hand cupped her jaw. "We've made a bargain. But there are no guarantees for a future unless we decide to unmask. Are you ready for the fantasy to end?"

The light died within her eyes, but she forced a smile. "I intend to enjoy these last nights with you. Because you make me happy."

Theo stared at her in astonishment. Her words and raw honesty humbled him. She'd always been his best friend, but now he realized the extent of how much she meant to him in every role.

Lover. Wife. Mother.

His.

Tomorrow night, she'd finally know the truth. Maybe she'd reject him. Maybe his bold move would ruin their friendship and she'd never forgive him. There was so much risk involved, but Theo had to follow this path to the end.

He pushed the disturbing thought aside and cradled her in his arms. "I can't argue with you. I love how direct you are."

"Why, have you met many women who aren't?"

He thought of his ex and how she'd betrayed him. All that time she'd held him to a higher standard, demanding perfection, when she was cheating the whole time. Theo was glad the wound had finally healed after all these years. Hailey had been the key to finally letting go of such bitterness, even though she still believed he held on to the betrayal. He wondered if she also used his past as an excuse to keep him in the category of friend, with no hope of crossing over. "Yes.

I've met women who lied and betrayed me. Women who pretend they want something they don't."

She reached out and ran her palm down his chest. Theo stilled and allowed her to touch him freely, exploring his abs, then moving downward. With one quick movement, her fingers grasped his dick, squeezing carefully. He sucked in a breath as he grew harder to the point of pain. Her actions contradicted her teasing tone. "I know exactly what I want. There's no pretending here."

He laughed. "And I want to give it to you. Over and over in as many different ways as I can. Maybe I should stop confessing my secrets and get back to our bargain."

He undressed them both and laid her on the bed. Immediately, she climbed on top of him, her fingers exploring his body with a frank curiosity he loved. He lay back and enjoyed the attention, savoring her ripe curves; the pink plump lips, the scent of vanilla and coconut drifting from her skin. Theo was greedy for her body but also wanted the intimacy of conversation while she lay naked in his arms.

"Name one guilty pleasure you never told anyone about."

She groaned and covered her face with her hands. Then peeked through her fingers. God, she was adorable. "I love art. I suck at painting and I can't draw a thing. I even tried to become an art investor but even my taste seemed awful. I bought a coloring book and a huge box of Crayola crayons. When I'm stressed, I color."

He drew back in surprise. "I never knew you did that."

She laughed. "Of course not, you don't know me."

Crap. He tried to hide his guilty expression and asked another quick question. "Tell one thing you hate. Something you never told anyone else."

She wrinkled her nose, obviously deep in thought. "Mansplaining. I work in the tech industry so I seem to always battle men who try to explain stuff to me I already know. And they do it in this condescending, patient way that

61

makes me crazy mad. But I've never admitted it to anyone. I'm afraid they may take it the wrong way, like I'm not being a team member. Stupid, right?"

"No. I can only imagine how you're treated differently because you're a woman." He thought over the times Hailey had seemed upset after a big meeting, but she'd never shared the real reason. Theo made a mental note to try and be more supportive on the job for her and everyone who worked underneath him.

"Any other questions?" she asked, lips pursed as she waited.

"Sexual fantasy?"

He loved the slow, sexy smile that made his heart stop. In one swift motion, she straddled him. Hailey arched her back, breasts thrust forward, rosy nipples tight and hard. She grasped his dick in her hand, fingers teasing the tip, eliciting drops of moisture. Red fiery waves fell down around her shoulders, and she gave a low laugh, her eyes full of secrets and passion and mystery.

"My sexual fantasy, Phantom?" Her tongue slid over her ripe bottom lip as if she imagined how he would taste. His breath hissed through his teeth as hunger ripped through him. "*This* is my fantasy. What I'm about to do right now. I want to take you in my mouth and make you scream my name. I want you inside me, so hard and fast that you forget every other woman you've been with. Since I promised I'd do anything you want, I'm begging for permission." Her voice dropped to a husky purr. "Will you let me suck you?"

He swore and clawed for control. His dick throbbed against the soft skin of her fingers as she continued teasing him, running her thumb over the turgid flesh. She had become his own personal sex slave, and now he was at her mercy. The excitement built as he gave her his answer. "I think I can allow it."

"Good. Now shut up."

Her breasts pressed against his chest as she lowered her head, and her tongue delicately licked at his flat male nipples. They hardened into little points, and then she used her teeth to gently pull, moving slowly down his chest, following the dark line of hair past his stomach.

Theodore groaned as her taut-tipped nipples caused a delicious friction against his skin. This was no longer his innocent, guarded Hailey. This was a sexual witch who used her nails and teeth and tongue to explore every inch of his body, as if crazy for the scent and taste of him. Her hands cupped his hips as she settled over his hard length, and then knelt between his legs.

She looked up once from her position. Gave a smug, half smile. Then lowered her head.

Her warm breath struck him first, and she opened her lips to take him in the slick, satin depths of her mouth. She teased him mercilessly, never taking his whole cock. Her tongue swirled around the tip, gathering the drops of moisture that spilled, then moved up and down the ridged underside as if he was a sweet lollipop she had discovered and decided to suck slowly.

Just as if his control was about to break, her hands cupped his balls and her lips opened wide to plunge him to the back of her throat.

He cursed.

The pleasure was too intense. Her tongue swirled around as her mouth held him tightly, moving in and out with a steady pace that tested his control. Her name spilled from his lips in a chant, and her suction grew even harder, luring him over the edge. She made hungry sounds in the back of her throat, as if she couldn't get enough of him, and his cock grew even harder within her wet mouth, the pressure building to a screaming point until he exploded in a sharp burst. She took it all. Her hair formed a silken curtain that swung back and forth over his thighs. Her tongue licked every last drop, then kept going until he swelled again and damned her to eternity.

He reached for her, but she avoided his movement. Desperate need heated his veins even after his climax.

"Tell me what you want," she urged. "Give me every detail."

He cursed, recognizing his own little game had been switched on him. His voice came out in a raspy groan. "Take my cock and put it inside your sweet, hot pussy. Ride me hard. I want to see your tits bounce as you come all over me."

She laughed low but he recognized the flare of lust in her blue eyes. "Beg me."

With one swift movement, he lifted her up and plunged his cock into her hot, slippery wetness. She gasped.

"I'm begging you, Hailey," he said.

She arched upward and took him to the hilt. Her legs spread wider to accommodate every inch of him. Her sweet cries spilled from her lips, obviously lost in sensation.

She rode him in a wild frenzy. Her hair streamed down her back; her heavy breasts bounced as she took everything he could give her. Her pussy clenched around him each time he drove inward, then clung madly in a rush of dampness as he withdrew.

He felt her wiggle toward the ultimate release and decided to tease. As he thrust into her, he kept his cock away from her swollen clit that would give her what she needed. His hands pulled and rubbed at her nipples, rolling the tips in his fingers until she begged him in low, frantic tones of arousal.

"Please, help me."

"How bad do you want it?" Again he plunged deep, keeping her inches away from the edge. He loved the way she looked as he fucked her, loved the way she gave him everything she had and demanded he keep up with her.

She rode him faster and her hips shimmied frantically. "I

need you." She panted, her blue eyes dazed with passion. "I need you."

The words reached out like a fist and tore into his gut. Hailey had changed him; opened him up;, and Theo wondered if he'd ever be the same. He rubbed his thumb over her swollen clit, pressing and rotating in the exact pressure she craved.

He drove inside of her. Again. And again. Then...

Hailey screamed. He felt her drench him, and he came again with her, emptying himself with a shout. She collapsed over his body like a rag doll, her hair spilling over his chest, her breathing rough and uneven.

"Damn, woman," he finally managed. "Any time you have another sexual fantasy, I'll be glad to help you out."

She laughed. "Donating your body to charity, huh?"

"It's a tough job but someone has to do it."

"I don't think I'll be able to walk tomorrow," she said.

He frowned. "Are you sore?"

"My thighs are still trembling."

He caressed her with soothing strokes. "As soon as I can get up, I'll run us a bath. That will take the aches away."

"I'm not complaining."

"It's for my own selfish pleasure. I want to show you the amazing things you can do underwater."

"I'll need a cane tomorrow."

He didn't answer. The realization of the end of their affair dangled before him with haunting urgency. Almost as if she knew his thoughts, she interlaced his fingers with her own and studied their hands. Fingers touching, pale skin against ivory. Entwined.

"I don't want this to be over," she whispered.

Hope bloomed, but he fought the emotion back. Theo refused to wonder what their last night would bring. The only thing in his power was to give her as much of himself as possible, and hope it was enough.

"I'll run the bath." He got up from the bed and disappeared into the bathroom.

Hailey lay back on the pillows and tried not to focus on his lackluster response. Her emotions may be real, but it could still be a game to him. Even though he'd obviously been scared and developed feelings, there was no guarantee he'd want to continue their relationship.

Bringing this masquerade into the real world may never work and Hailey needed to be real. She was falling in love with him, but he could view her as a novelty. A short-term, intense affair never meant to be more. At least, if she chose to walk away, she'd have the memories to take with her. Their time together was a gift. She refused to see it any other way.

Hailey followed him into the bathroom. The scents of jasmine and lavender rose to her nostrils. The mirrors steamed deliciously and wrapped them both in a world unto their own making. She quietly shut the door behind her and stood before him, naked.

He reached his hand out. With a smile, she took it, and they stepped into the tub. The sharp sting of the hot water made her gasp slightly, before she steeped below the surface. He positioned her so she floated over him, her buttocks pressed between his spread legs, her back lay against his chest. She sighed in deep contentment as he took the soap and rubbed it between his hands.

Slowly, he began soaping her shoulders, digging his thumbs into the sore muscles. A moan rose from her lips. His hands were slippery with bubbles as he worked on the tendons in her neck and moved downward—the line of her spine, her upper arms, and slid around to cup her breasts. He played with the soft mounds, cupping bubbles and allowing them to float through the air, grazing the tips of her breasts like a wet, dainty kiss. He washed every part of her, lingered on every curve with a tenderness that made tears sting against her lids. Her eyes closed with dreamy pleasure as she gave him her body, the gift he had asked for. If only he knew her body hadn't been the only gift she entrusted to him.

She had given her heart.

Long, supple fingers slid around her hips and lingered over the full curve of her buttocks. Her cheeks tightened in anticipation as she felt him gently explore the cleft, parting her labia and softly touching her. Hailey floated; muscles melted like warm, sticky honey, helpless under his spell.

"Phantom, what are you doing to me?" she asked in wonder, eyes shut as she drank in every sensation. The bubbles teased her taut-tipped breasts and sloshed over her quickening muscles. Her cleft felt swollen, and the warm water mixed with her own juices until her thighs floated open and her sex was exposed to his gaze.

"God, you're stunning," he muttered. His fingers clenched into the full cheeks. "I just want to look at you." He drew her knees up so she lay open to him. "I want to take you again. I can't get enough of you, Hailey."

"I want you again, too," she whispered. "I want you to take me every way possible. I want to belong to you completely."

"You already do." He seemed surprised the words slipped out. "Don't you?"

"Yes."

She arched back. Her pussy was open and exposed to his hot gaze. "I have to taste you. Get on your knees and hold on to the edge of the tub."

She moved. Her fingers gripped the cold, white marble as she knelt on her knees. Her flesh quivered as the cool air rushed over her flesh. She felt his hard hands part her legs and urge her forward so her buttocks rose in the air, awaiting his next move.

Hailey felt his gaze on the curve of her buttocks; the hot pink of her cleft. He leaned over her and blew gently, and she jerked back in response, a half moan caught on her lips.

He lowered his head, and his teeth bit into her firm cheeks, testing her. He moved inward, squeezing, cupping, while his tongue snaked out to take quick, sharp licks. She wiggled helplessly against him but he only laughed and drew out the anticipation. The tip of his tongue slid into her pussy and licked with slow strokes. Her swollen flesh became sensitive to every stroke, and then he flicked his tongue against her over and over with hard, quick motions. Hailey cried out, but he still held back. His fingers pushed the firm globes of her flesh apart so he tasted all of her. His hot tongue teased her throbbing clit again, and again, until…

She came hard, pushing back with a cry. He grabbed her hips, dragged her up, and thrust inside her..

Heat.

Fullness.

Possession.

The convulsions seized her body and ripped through her. Caught in a whirlwind, she was helpless to do anything but ride out the wild wave of pleasure.

He fucked her with a savagery that claimed her as his. She took every inch of him, pussy tight and hot as he pushed even deeper, and she met him all the way, her body arched like a bow, quickening in response to his fierce thrusts. Water slapped over the tub in gentle waves. Bubbles floated through the air. And then her orgasm took hold like a savage fist that scooped her up and hurtled her toward the stars.

This time when he held her, Hailey didn't allow herself to think of tomorrow. She lay her head on his damp, muscled chest, spent for now, and wrapped her arms around him. His heart pounded in a steady rhythm against her ear.

The clock ticked. She roused herself enough to speak, still greedy to learn everything she could about the man in her arms. "What were you like as a boy, Phantom?"

"More secrets?"

Hailey smiled against him as she heard the teasing note in

his voice. "I want to know a little bit about you. As a man, you certainly know how to give a woman pleasure. Tell me about the boy."

He was silent for a few moments, but she waited, sensing he was ready to open up.

"I grew up very poor," he said. "My father ran out on my mother when I was seven. He found a local girl with no complications and they took off. That was the last time I heard from him. I was almost glad to see him go. Even at seven, I remember him yelling at my mother, hitting me occasionally. Telling me I was useless."

She kept her voice low and soothing, even though her heart squeezed in pain. "What did your mother do to support you?"

"Waitressed. Cleaned up after people in hotels. Anything to keep food on the table. I helped as much as I could, but it was years before I could earn any decent money."

She felt the coldness within him envelop the man who had shared the last three nights with her; the man who had laughed and teased and held her close. She held him tighter as if her body warmth could ward off the chill. "What did you like as a boy?"

"Things I could fix. Things I could control. Math, science, cars, computers."

"What business did you decide to embark on?

"Computers. One of my mother's boyfriends was decent to her, and loved to fool around on a laptop. He taught me a few things and something clicked."

"What?"

"I could finally control something. A computer has no emotions, and does what it's told. I decided I would learn everything. Coding. Hacking. Anything that can be done was a challenge for me." He shifted in the water and his hand played with the wet strands of her hair. "Eventually, I found a job at a computer firm and worked my way up.

Just like you, I took my opportunity and made the most of it."

"Do you ever think about your father?"

"No."

She picked up her head and gazed into his eyes. The gleaming white mask covered half of his face, but the burning light in his eyes confirmed he was a liar. Hailey stroked his hard cheek, traced the full line of his lower lip, then cradled his jaw. Tenderness bloomed within her.

"I was invited to the senior prom when I was eighteen," she said. "I had never been asked to a dance before, so I was beyond excitement. I spent hours looking through magazines for a dress, talking to my friends about which party we'd attend. When I told my parents I was invited, they refused to let me go." She paused, wrestling with the memories. "They informed me most teenagers lose their virginity during prom. I was better than that. I would not barter my body for a chance at a solid, successful future. So, I called my date and told him I got sick. I watched out my window as the limos pulled out of the driveways with kids dressed in gowns and tuxedos. And I hated them. I wished I could just be a normal teen-ager and kiss a boy for the first time on the night of prom. I was so tired of trying to be good, of trying to follow my parents' rules. I actually had a rebellion that night and screamed. Told them how much I hated them and their stupid restrictions. I went to sleep that night and wished they were dead." She took a deep breath and angled her head so he could see her face. "Years later they died. I was finally free. I turned my back on the past and vowed to never think about them again. I wanted to build a new life for myself."

"So, you won."

"Ask me, Phantom. Ask me if I think about them anymore."

"Do you?"

"Every day."

Understanding took hold and blossomed. The chill eased, and Hailey lowered her mouth and kissed him. Her tongue slipped inside to give and share and receive. He tasted of brandy and smoke and male hunger. He tasted of her essence. And she knew in that moment she loved him.

Hailey broke off the kiss as the realization shook her in a storm of fear. Their gazes locked, and then the ringing of the bell in the distance cut through the air, and the moment was gone.

Slowly, Hailey eased away from him. God, she didn't want to leave.

SLOWLY, THEO EASED AWAY FROM HER. GOD, HE DIDN'T WANT to leave.

"Phantom?"

"Yes?"

"Besides computers, what did you really love when you were little? What made you happy?"

He studied her face. Damned if she didn't know how to reach into a man's chest and rip his heart out. With that simple question, instead of focusing on the rage and pain of his childhood, he remembered something he thought he'd forgotten. A smile played about his lips as the memory took hold.

"Roses." He shook his head, almost embarrassed. "We had this neighbor who used to garden. She had fruits, vegetables, herbs. And flowers, incredible rose bushes in red and pink and yellow. She was nice to me. When my mother was entertaining her boyfriends, she would invite me to her house and fix me peanut butter and banana sandwiches, and I would stare out at the roses."

His vision blurred as vivid colors and fragrances danced

before him. When his gaze re-focused, he realized she had given him a precious gift.

His one good memory.

She smiled, then leaned over to kiss him good-bye.

"Until tomorrow," she whispered.

She rose from the tub and shut the door behind her.

Theodore sat in the cooled water for a long time after she had gone and thought about her smile. Thought about tomorrow.

Their final night.

CHAPTER SEVEN

THEODORE WATCHED her walk up the twisting pathway. She wore a long, dark cloak with a hood that absorbed the shadows, and hid her fiery red hair as she made her way into the house. The music and laughter were deafening; the sexual orgies and encounters flooded through the rooms as they approached their final encounter.

He paced the room with long, graceful strides. His black robe flowed behind him. He still wore the mask, would wear it until the final hour of the clock, and then she would know his identity. Would she draw back with shock and disgust? Would she throw away the moments they experienced these past nights because he was flesh and blood, and not her billionaire fantasy? Did she want to continue this relationship? Did she have feelings for him – the real him - her best friend Theodore?

He cursed violently. One last night to touch and taste her sweet body. To kiss her lips and claim her for his own. One last time until the truth was revealed and she made her decision.

The door opened. Her scent beckoned him, a twist of

vanilla and coconut that swirled around his senses and got him hard immediately. She stepped in and closed the door behind her.

Then loosened her cloak and let it fall to the floor in soft, velvet folds.

He sucked in his breath.

She was naked. Her glorious red hair tumbled down her back and shoulders, playing peek-a-boo with rosy pink nipples. Her breasts were full and creamy white. Her long legs framed an inviting center of curls that hid her sex. Beneath the sweet scent he caught the undertones of female arousal.

She wore no mask.

His gaze greedily took in every familiar feature. The graceful curve of her jaw and cheek; the arching red brows; the red lips. Her Caribbean blue eyes flickered warily but she stood before him in all her glory, daring him to turn away.

He closed the distance between them. Thrusting his fingers within the fire of her hair, he lifted her face up and gazed deeply into her eyes.

"You're beautiful."

Then his mouth took hers.

It was a kiss of raw hunger and demand; a need to possess and be possessed; a vow to give pleasure and to take. Her lips opened under his, her tongue tangling, thrusting as they drank from one another.

Her hands slipped around his shoulders as his lips closed around her tongue and sucked, drawing her very essence into him. His teeth sunk into her ripe lower lip, taking love bites, and he trailed kisses across her cheek, exploring every feature that had been hidden by the mask.

When he lifted his head, her eyes burned as if with fever. Her nails dug fiercely into his shoulders.

"Take me, Phantom. Take me now. I belong to you."

He lifted her up and they tumbled to the bed. There was no teasing, no love play, as she ripped off his robe and ran her hands over his long, lean body.

They were ravenous for each other; hands and tongues and lips tangled together. He cupped her buttocks and sucked on her nipples as she reached down and took his throbbing cock between her fingers and squeezed.

She wrapped her legs around his hips and they rolled over in the cool, satin sheets. Then she climbed on top of him, grasped his cock, and impaled herself with one smooth push.

He groaned. She gasped.

She arched back so he buried himself to the hilt in her tight, clingy heat. He sat up on the bed and wrapped his arms around her so they were face to face, flesh buried within flesh, gazes locked. Her nipples pressed into his chest. His lips hungrily took hers and plunged inside her mouth as deeply as his cock. He rocked his hips. Once. Again.

She cried out as convulsions shook her body. The orgasm overtook her.

He shouted her name and followed her over. Her teeth savagely sunk into his shoulder as she clung to him.

Hailey slid down from the pinnacle with his cock still buried inside of her. Her flesh pulsed and quivered in tiny vibrations and she turned her head to press kisses over his mouth, enjoying his ragged warm breaths against her mouth. Her fingers gentled and stroked back his silky, black hair, then lingered over the gleaming smoothness of his mask which still hid him from her full view.

"I can't get enough of you," she whispered, then nipped at his bottom lip. His mouth curved upward in a smile. "Would you like to know another one of my fantasies?"

A deep chuckle rumbled his chest. "If it's anything like the last one, they'll be carrying me out on a stretcher."

She licked at his jaw and tasted clean soap and the salty tang of male sweat. His rough stubble prickled against her tongue.

"Never. You're my new superhero. No Viagra ever needed. Hours of pleasure guaranteed, until a woman begs for mercy."

"What is this superhero called?"

"Studman."

He laughed. "Batman. Superman. Spiderman. Now Studman."

"Exactly. Still want to hear my fantasy?"

"Go ahead."

"I lock you in a room and take away your clothes. You're at my command every hour of the day, completely at my mercy, and you'll do anything I ask. The only way to escape is to please me, so you work very hard at it."

"Hmmm. Sounds like what we're doing now except I'm the one who has to obey."

"Exactly."

"Hailey?"

"Yes?"

"That's my sexual fantasy, too."

She laughed with him, snuggling into his arms, her fingers playing with the swirling dark hairs on his chest. "There's one other part in my fantasy I forgot to mention."

"You have whips and chains."

"No, but I may have to add that one in later."

"What is it?"

"You have no mask."

He grew silent. The sounds of the party drifted up the stairwell and reminded them of the short hours left. "Once I remove my mask, the game is over. I want a little more time with you."

She blinked back sudden tears, and concentrated on the

moment, wanting to pull every second of pleasure from the man beneath her.

"Then take it, Phantom. Take me over and over until the bell rings."

His eyes blazed with promise. "I intend to."

He rained kisses over her face, naked from the removal of her mask. She shook slightly and knew no other man had every taken her body and soul like her Phantom.

"Give me a little more on our last night together, Hailey," he said.

She tossed him a wicked smile. "I thought I already did."

He chuckled. "I mean truth. Tell me what you want from your life. Tell me what you still fear."

This time, when she spoke she had no mask to hide herself. This time, she didn't need one. She already spoke to the man she loved, and refused to hide anything. Hailey wanted to tell him the only thing she wanted was him, but he asked the question with the assumption this was their final meeting.

"I want to build something that lasts," she said softly. "Don't all people want the same thing? Someone to remember them. If I can't do it with children or the love of my life, I'll pick friendship. I'll pick rewarding work that makes a difference."

He waited a while before answering. "If you had a chance to have this love of your life, would you be strong enough to reach out for him?

"Yes." She spoke the truth. Ciro Demitris had given her that gift.

"And your fear?"

"You already erased my fears, Phantom. The only thing left to be afraid of is being without you."

He turned from her then, as if he couldn't bear the emotion of looking into her face. Hailey took the time to ask her own questions. "And you? What do you fear?"

His voice came from a distant place. "I fear the truth," he said. With one quick movement, he rolled over and pinned her to the mattress. "But you're here now. Mine for the next few hours. That's all I need."

Then his mouth took hers.

The evening slid by with slow strokes of the clock, as they roused one another to make love through the night. He took her places she had never seen before. She showed him a tenderness and emotion he had never felt before. The bed became their escape from the world beyond, as the full moon shimmered in the sky and the sounds of the party rose and fell through the rooms. And when the bell finally chimed at dawn; when the music and laughter and screams grew to a crescendo, he sat up in bed and looked at her naked body.

"It's time, Hailey."

His eyes were filled with resolve, and another emotion she couldn't put a name to. A glint; a glimmer; something she needed to hold onto but was too afraid to demand from him. Did he love her? Would he walk away without a second thought? Was she just another woman involved in his masquerade, a rousing distraction to never be thought of again?

She sat up. Heart pounding wildly against her chest, she waited.

He reached up and with one savage motion, ripped his mask off.

Hailey sucked in her breath as she stared at the man before her. The man she knew. The man who had played a game and betrayed her trust.

Theodore Rivers.

She watched in shocked silence as he dipped his head and popped out the contact lenses. Then he reached up and rubbed his fingers through his hair. The strands fell over his face as they had so many times in the past. The diamond in his left ear winked like a beacon signaling his deceit. His brown eyes gazed into hers with a steadiness that prevented her from turning away. And suddenly, his voice and scent and touch made sense, and she gasped as the pain shook through her body.

"Why?" she moaned. "Theo, why would you do this to me?"

He flinched at the accusation. His voice was low and urgent. "Hailey, you have to listen to me. If you decide you never want to see me again, I can accept the consequences. But this was my only chance, a chance of a lifetime, and I'll never have a regret about taking it."

Her eyes widened at his words, and she bit down on her lower lip to stop from crying out. The room spun around her, but she forced herself to remain on the bed and listen. Even if it was for the last time.

"When we first met, I only wanted your friendship. I was still recovering from my wife, but you filled a part of me I've never really known before. I felt comfortable and accepted with another woman for the first time. But as our friendship developed, I fell in love with you. Every part. I loved seeing you in baggy sweat pants with no make-up. I loved watching the basketball games together and taking you out to dinner. I even love all those habits of yours no one is supposed to know about. You sing opera when you clean, and panic if you don't brush your teeth four times a day, and insist on walking in the back door instead of the front because you're superstitious."

"Theodore— "

He put up a hand and forged on. "I watched you every day with an ache in my gut because I knew you wouldn't give me a chance. I listened to you complain about your looks when all I wanted to do was yank you in my arms and prove how beautiful I thought you were. And I wanted more, Hailey, so much more. I wanted to give you pleasure until you screamed my name. I wanted to explore every deep fantasy you ever had and some of my own. But whenever I made a move, you backed away. There was no way to cross the line." He took a deep breath and continued. "When you told me about the masquerade party and Demitris, I knew I could lose you. It was the opportunity of a lifetime. Finally, you would see me as a man, not your best friend. I wanted to be both. I needed you to see all of me, because I already loved all of you."

"Theodore—"

She tried to say more but he didn't stop; just kept talking with a desperation and intensity like he was battling the tick of the clock to change their ending.

"I want to marry you. Have babies. Work together, play together, I want it all. I want to take you to bed every night and make sure your knees buckle every time I kiss you. Everything I said this weekend was the truth. I only hid my face. My heart's been open to you for the past few years."

Her body trembled helplessly from the onslaught of words and emotions. The room finally fell silent, and she drew in a ragged breath, trying to make sense of what he had told her. This was Theodore, her best friend and confidante. But he was also Ciro Demitris, a phantom figure who kissed her breathlessly and set her body on fire.

Hailey closed her eyes. A rush of images whizzed before her. The comfort in his presence. The way he made her laugh. The burning edge in his eyes when he looked at her. The facts were all there, had always been there, but she had refused to face them.

And suddenly, a blinding flash of realization shook her to the core. This was what she had been afraid of. She had chased after a strange man this weekend and convinced herself she had been lacking excitement and adventure. In reality, Theodore had always been the one she ran from. The man she could share her life with. She stubbornly built a wall around the possibility there could be more between them, afraid of the truth.

This was the man she loved.

Hailey opened her eyes. Her best friend stood a few inches away, his familiar features twisted with an agony that tore at her heart. Tears spilled over her lids as the knowledge sunk in. He'd always loved her. Loved her enough to take the risk of losing her completely by setting up the entire charade. Loved her enough to wait until he thought she was ready.

His gaze registered her acceptance and the tears that streamed down her cheek. With a low mutter, he closed the distance between them and took her into his arms.

His mouth claimed her for his own. His hot tongue thrust inside and she gave it all back wholeheartedly. When he finally lifted his head, Theo smiled.

"You forgive me for not allowing you to meet your rich tycoon?"

She laughed in delight and threw her arms around him. "Who needs a tycoon? He probably has no idea how to do his own laundry."

Dark brown eyes gleamed with intensity. "This wasn't just a weekend fling, Hailey. All the things I did to you, with you, I intend to continue. And I have a long list of fantasies."

He backed her up until her knees hit the edge of the bed. Slowly, she lay back and parted her legs. Then smiled. "How long?"

"Oh, enough to last the next twenty years."

"Maybe we should get started."

"Maybe we should."

Theo climbed on the bed and pressed his body to hers. Dragged her thighs apart so she was open to his gaze. Then thrust into her wet heat, his beloved face watching her fall apart under each delicious stroke.

"Theodore."

She watched his eyes darken with pleasure as his name echoed through the air. And Hailey gave herself completely over to the man she loved.

The man she had always loved.

THE END

WANT MORE?

Want to receive an exclusive bonus scene from the Unbound series? Grab it here along with a free book!
Claim it here: https://BookHip.com/MZQNJJZ

OR scan the QR code below:

ABOUT THE AUTHOR

Jennifer Probst wrote her first book at twelve years old. She bound it in a folder, read it to her classmates, and hasn't stopped writing since. She holds a masters in English Literature and lives in the beautiful Hudson Valley in upstate New York.

She is the New York Times, USA Today, and Wall Street Journal bestselling author of over fifty books in contemporary romance fiction.. She was thrilled her book, The Marriage Bargain, spent 26 weeks on the New York Times. Her work has been translated in over a dozen countries, sold over a million copies, and was dubbed a "romance phenom" by Kirkus Reviews.

She loves hearing from readers, visit her website at www.jenniferprobst.com.

Sign up for her newsletter at www.jenniferprobst.com/subscribe for a free book!

www.ingramcontent.com/pod-product-compliance
Lightning Source LLC
Chambersburg PA
CBHW031856170626
46807CB00004B/1749